The
Cheshire Cheese Cat

A DICKENS OF A TALE

The
Cheshire Cheese Cat

A DICKENS OF A TALE

Carmen Agra Deedy & Randall Wright

Drawings by Barry Moser

SCHOLASTIC INC.

ISBN 978-0-545-50126-2

12 11 10 9 8 7 6 5 4 3   13 14 15 16 17/0

Printed in the U.S.A.   40

First Scholastic printing, September 2012

Book design and composition by Barry Moser, with Loraine M. Joyner

DEDICATIONS

To my luminous granddaughter, Ruby Rabbit

—C. D.

To Dawn, my sunshine and joy

—R. W.

For my friend Helen Casey-Brazeau and her Miss Bailey

—B. M.

ACKNOWLEDGMENTS

The authors wish to thank the following for helping turn this book into a reality:

Our dear spouses, John and Dawn, for their patience, their advice, and the many hearty meals.

Our friend Rohan Bayer-Fox for ensuring that these two presumptuous Yanks didn't go too far afield. Any errors found herein are entirely our own.

Fellow wordsmith Rick Walton for providing just the right touch of Dickensian inspiration.

Our most splendid and Pippish editors, Vicky Holifield and Margaret Quinlin.

Friends who generously read and commented on the manuscript: Tersi Bendiburg, Paula Lepp, Susan Rapaport, Dea North, and Bill Harley.

The Ravenmaster at the Tower of London for the fascinating glimpse into the world of ravens.

The Decatur Library for its excellent reference section and knowledgeable staff.

And Ye Olde Cheshire Cheese, of course, for inspiring this whole business on a misty London night in 2002, while in the company of Kates, Erin, and Lauren.

SKILLEY—*A jaded street cat with a disgraceful secret and a shameful past.*

PINCH—*A perfectly foul villain and Skilley's nemesis.*

YE OLDE CHESHIRE CHEESE—*This venerable inn is one of the grand ladies of London public houses. For centuries, she has attracted writers and word lovers the likes of Samuel Johnson, Mark Twain, and Arthur Conan Doyle. And cats. Let's not forget the cats...*

PIP—*A mouse of Ye Olde Cheshire Cheese with more than a few secrets of his own.*

NELL—*The innkeeper's misunderstood daughter, who dotes on the inn's animals.*

CROOMES—*The temperamental cook whose cheese is famous far and wide; she is often in a state of ill temper.*

MR. CHARLES DICKENS—*A writer of some distinction who frequents the inn.*

HENRY—*The portly innkeeper, who is desperate to rid his inn of cheese-thieving mice.*

ADELE—*A barmaid, busybody, and hater of mice.*

MALDWYN—*The proud creature hidden away in the inn's garret, upon whom rests the future of the realm.*

A MYSTERIOUS VISITOR—*You didn't really expect a description, did you?*

CHAPTER ONE

HE WAS THE BEST OF TOMS. He was the worst of toms.

Fleet of foot, sleek and solitary, Skilley was a cat among cats. Or so he would have been, but for a secret he had carried since his early youth. A secret that caused him to live in hidden shame, avoiding even casual friendship lest anyone discover—

"Scat, cat!" A broom came down hard out of London's cold and fog. Startled, Skilley leapt sideways and the broom whiffled empty air.

The cat, however, refused to scat.

He eyed the dead fish, then the broom, calculating the distance between the two.

"Off now, you thieving moggy!" the fishmonger shrilled. As if reading his thoughts, she kicked the fish under her stall and cocked the broom for another swing.

Angry women with brooms unnerved him. The only encounter Skilley dreaded more was one with Pinch, the terror of Fleet Street.

With a flick of his peculiar tail, Skilley turned his back to the fishwife, putting all the disdain he could muster into the sway of his hips.

But once he had rounded the corner, he flitted into an alley, where he ran its length with darts and dashes. Pausing at the end of the passageway, he surveyed the familiar cobblestones and his spirits lightened.

Huddled over her fire, on a near corner, was the crone who sold roasted chestnuts for a ha-penny. A few paces from her, a boy hawked mulled cider. Down the street, the song of the rag and bone man mingled with the rattle of carriages and the hum of pedestrians.

Ah, Fleet Street, Skilley thought.

Home to some of the finest eating and drinking in London, the street was a perfect gathering place for scavengers. And down a certain modest court stood a most particular pub, famed as a haunt for London writers: Ye Olde Cheshire Cheese.

Skilley peered through the gauzy mist. The inn's hanging

wooden sign twitched in a swirl of January wind. Skilley shivered and looked longingly toward the cozy tavern.

There has to be a way in, he thought.

"Whatever it is you're thinkin'—don't," came the warning, followed by a soft, dangerous purr.

"Ah, Pinch." Skilley's tone was pleasant, but this outward calm belied the clenching of his stomach. "And a fine day to you."

Cold-blooded and volatile, Pinch was not a cat to be trifled with. "You can keep your *ah, Pinch* and your *fine day.*" His eyes narrowed and the hackles on his ginger-striped shoulders rose in challenge. "Just mind you keep away from The Cheese."

"The Cheese?" Skilley asked, unblinking. "What of it?"

"Mice," Pinch said.

"Mice?" Skilley's eyes widened with pretend innocence.

"Aye, mice. The Cheese tavern is overrun with 'em."

"Ah."

"Grandest cheese in England, or so they say. And where there's that manner of cheese, there's mice aplenty." He paused and gave a pleasurable groan. "Fat and juicy. Plump and round, young and…tender." His nose twitched as though it could already smell a nest of baby mice.

"Mice aplenty, you say?" Skilley interrupted.

"The tavern is my 'ome. You 'old your distance."

Skilley sat and licked a paw, a token of his indifference. As an added touch, he stroked behind his ear. "I wasn't aware you had a home, Pinch."

"Aye, but I do. And that there's it." He nodded toward the inn.

"Hmmm, odd that," said Skilley. "A cozy tavern for a home, and yet here you sit on the icy cobblestones passing the day with the likes of me."

"Well, it will be my 'ome soon, you watch and see. The place is ate up with mice, and the master's witless for want of a mousekiller."

"The Cheese is looking for a mouser?" A not-unpleasant chill danced up Skilley's spine.

"Yes, and I'm it. Cross me and s'elp me I'll rip out your..."

But Skilley had dropped the thread

of the conversation. A mouser, eh? A plan began to nibble at his mind—a plan of such elegant simplicity he was amazed he hadn't thought of it before.

Stretching lazily, he rose, and with a last twitch of his crooked tail said, "You are a cat among cats, Pinch, and I thank you!"

"For what?" the ginger cat snarled after him. "What'd I do?"

Skilley didn't answer. He was already engrossed in the audacity of a scheme so bold, so cunning, it would surely set him up for the rest of his nine lives.

CHAPTER TWO

Cat...

               Cat...

         Cat...

             Cat...

Cat...

                   Cat...

"What do you hear?"

"Pip! Tell us what they're say—"

"Shhhh." Pip raised a single digit on his tiny paw and pressed it to his lips. His fellow mice fell begrudgingly silent.

Pip closed his eyes and pressed a fuzzy, delicate ear to the thin wall between himself and the chop room of Ye Olde Cheshire Cheese. To his dismay, the wall was not thin enough. He could catch only a word or two, which made it difficult, even for him, to understand the language of the humans.

Human language was a talent he had mastered while living in the pocket of Nell, the innkeeper's daughter.

As Pip strained to listen, his thoughts returned to that blackest of days when his entire family, including five brothers and sisters, had been cruelly murdered by some unknown hand.

Croomes the cook. Pip harbored no doubt there. *Her bloody cleaver was found nearby, was it not?*

Pip alone had been left alive—unseen, no doubt, due to his unusually small size. Nell had heard his squeaks and rescued him from the bloody carnage. Her anger and distress was such that her breath came in gasps as she carried him away up, up, up the twisting, winding, impossible stairs of the inn.

She'd stopped only when she reached the safety of the attic. Holding the frightened little thing in one cupped hand, she'd used the other to search and find the bag of lamb's wool. She'd torn away a small cloud of it, pressed it deep into her apron pocket, and then, with much tenderness, she'd nestled Pip safely inside.

When she heard his hiccuped sobs, Nell's anger melted away, replaced with a welling up of grief that was as much for herself as for the mouse.

Nell's mother had not experienced a violent death. Quite the opposite. Her passing had followed a short and rather unremarkable illness. Still, there had been no proper good-bye. Her young mother had simply fallen asleep and never again awakened, like some princess in an ancient tale. Nell and her father were left feeling as though she'd never really gone, as though they might yet encounter her suddenly on a stair.

Everyone agreed that Nell had not been the same since that day. The less charitable among the inn's inhabitants went so far as to suggest she had gone a bit soft in the head.

Whether Nell were sane, daft, or merely heartsick, the young mouse had found a friend in the newly orphaned girl. Reaching into her pocket, she'd stroked his downy back with a fingertip and whispered, "You sleep now. No one will hurt you, so long as you're with me."

And she'd choked back a sob.

It had been the best and worst day of Pip's life.

That is, until this afternoon, when he finally quieted his fellow creatures enough to hear spoken again, in the rumbling voice of the innkeeper, that ominous word...

Cat.

CHAPTER THREE

The moment Skilley left Pinch's side, he set his plan in motion. Careful to seem unhurried lest his rival might be watching, Skilley wove a path among the bustling humans until he lost himself in the crowd. He waited but a few moments. Then, with a leap and a lightning sprint, he sped to the unimposing front door of Ye Olde Cheshire Cheese. Not to the back door, mind you, where smelly fish bones and gelatinous puddings were hurled daily into the gutter—and where no doubt, even now, Pinch and the other toms and tabbies would be assembling for the evening meal.

No. Skilley marched directly to the front door.

Unthinkable impudence for a cat.

Halted by a brief moment of doubt—not in the plan itself, but in its execution, he paused. It was a perfect plan that was now perfectly ruined by…a door.

Of all things.

Skilley hated doors.

He sat back on his haunches and considered the situation.

He looked at his right paw.

Then his left.

He examined the confounding doorknob. While he stared, as if in answer to his unspoken wish, a gloved hand reached out from the fog and pushed open the door.

"Good evening, Sir Puss," said the owner of the hand. His voice sounded like the rolling bass notes of the great pipe organ at Saint Paul's Cathedral.

Skilley ignored the greeting and darted inside. The man and his companion followed close behind. "A slab of cheese and a loaf, Henry," the first cried to the landlord. "Mr. Collins is feeling a bit peckish this afternoon." He pulled a leather-bound notebook from the pocket of his greatcoat and set it on a table.

"And who's this with you?" Henry asked.

"Why, you know my friend, Wilkie! He's just penned a work that will take London by storm. It's about a ghostly woman in white—"

"Writers," Henry sighed. "No, I meant old tom there." The innkeeper tilted his head in the direction of the cat.

As all eyes turned upon him, Skilley shot back the most ill-tempered expression he could muster, hoping to impress them with his sincere ferocity.

"Just another loyal patron for The Cheese," said Mr. Collins with a laugh and a respectful bow toward Skilley. "Give him a slice of your best, Henry."

The gentleman of the musical voice swept off his hat and cloak and hung them on a peg. "Perhaps he's heard of your troubles and wants to recommend himself as rat catcher. He has a fierce enough look about him."

The man's words seemed serious, but the tone made Skilley think that laughter lay not far behind.

I'll have to keep my eye on this one, he thought.

"MOUSE catcher, if you please, sir," corrected Henry, lowering his voice. "There're no rats at The Cheese, sir, Providence be praised! Though enough mice to drive Adele to hysterics and my poor little Nell to near madness! Since Croomes came to our kitchen these ten winters ago, our Cheshire cheese is finer than ever, and it would seem every mouse in London who's got wind of it has come to claim his share." Henry heaved a great sigh of consternation. He turned to Skilley. "Let's see here, then, *mouse* catcher."

The innkeeper bent forward, hands on knees, and inspected Skilley with a critical eye. London's alleyways, docks, and sewers appeared to have dealt harshly with the young cat. The artful dodging of hansom cabs, chamber pots, and the inevitable fishwives' brooms had left him with a ragged ear, numerous scrapes, and a tracery of scars.

Then there was the hooked tail; it looked to have once been painfully broken—but by what?

"A right cruel-looking puss," Henry said at last. "But can he catch mice, Mr. Dickens?"

The great writer, however, was no longer listening. He had settled himself in a corner where he'd begun a vigorous scribbling in his notebook—scribbling and crossing out, scribbling and crossing out, unaware of those around him.

"Don't mind him," Mr. Collins said, nodding toward Mr. Dickens. "He's in a right state. Says he'll never write again."

"What? Never write again?"

"All for want of a beginning," Mr. Collins answered. "The first edition of his new magazine is coming out soon, but poor Charles seems to be at a loss for an opening to his story." Then he answered Henry's question about the cat. "If the look of that tom is anything to judge by, Henry, I pity your poor mice."

Skilley rewarded Mr. Collins with a low growl.

From behind the wall, through the tiniest of cracks, with ever mounting alarm, a pewter gray mouse watched and listened.

~~Those were dire days, indeed~~
The times were ~~cruel~~
~~ghastly~~
~~appalling~~
 It was the worst of all the days the world has seen—

Oh, why can't I write an opening for my new novel that stands out from all the rest?

I'm at Ye Olde Cheshire Cheese today with my friend Wilkie. I was looking forward to a marvelous afternoon of cheese and chummery, but with my well of words tapped dry, I can only despair. If only I could find my opening as effortlessly as old Henry has found his mouser . . .

I think I'll just jump in the Thames.
Or become a lamplighter or a chimney sweep.
Anything but a writer.

CHAPTER FOUR

Pip licked his paw,
      flicked his ear,
            licked his paw.
He smoothed his gray fur,
            licked his paw…

A good washing always helped him think.

This situation was unraveling quickly. He'd seen it happen with a shawl once—a fine silk wrap worn by an elegant lady who had left the upstairs dining room in a rush. As she'd hastened through the chop room, her shawl had snagged on a nail that some ancient workman had left exposed in a baseboard. Pip had watched in fascination as a long, thin thread of indigo blue trailed the woman out of the pub, down the court, and around the corner.

That was precisely the sort of feeling this cat gave him.

Things were unraveling.

"We've outlasted two fires, countless monarchs, and the plague," he reassured himself. "We can survive a cat."

But *whatever shall we do with Maldwyn?* came the niggling afterthought.

He peeked through the crack again. The cat certainly looked dangerous, though there was something about his eyes that puzzled Pip—a hint of something out of place. But he had little time for puzzles now.

It was time to act.

Without stopping to think any further, Pip hurried off to call a meeting of the mouse council. No—he must call a full meeting of the mouse citizenry! And he would be forced to use the ancient signal. The quickest route obliged him to pass directly beneath the feet of two patrons who'd just settled down to a fine repast of bread, pickles, and cheese.

Catching a whiff of Cheshire, Pip's highly refined nostrils betrayed him, and he paused for a single fateful instant.

And that was to prove unfortunate.

CHAPTER FIVE

Skilley surveyed the setting before him: men, meal, and mouse. With the patience of a natural predator, he held back.

Not yet.

Wait.

It was essential that the innkeeper see him.

He steeled himself, and then executed a perfect pounce and snatch.

"Lookie 'ere," cried Adele, a barmaid. "Why, 'e got 'im!"

"Got who?" asked the innkeeper, who had missed the whole thing after all.

"Got a bloomin' mouse, 'at's 'oo!" The barmaid clapped her hands and bounced up on her toes.

"Ah," said Mr. Collins, helping himself to a slice of cheese. "Well done."

The innkeeper looked about, confused by the shouting.

Skilley strutted across the floor, letting the mouse's long tail dangle from his mouth in plain view.

"It would appear that you've secured yourself a mouser," said Mr. Dickens.

At last Henry caught on. The bowlegged (practically parenthetical) figure of a man rocked back and forth as his face split into a broad grin. "So it would seem, Mr. Dickens, sir, so it would seem."

CHAPTER SIX

Dark and damp.

And—ouch—what sharp teeth!

Caught, but still alive, Pip's heart pounded.

Instinctively, the little mouse employed the last desperate strategy of the weak. He played dead.

But...*what was that smell?*

No time for that thought now. Pip forced himself to remain limp, despite the pressing threat of the cat's teeth around his thin belly.

Then came a jump.

And a jolt.

Followed by a thumping descent.

His tormentor carried him—where? Down the stairs? And then, just as suddenly as he had been captured, he was rudely spat out onto the stone floor.

Pip lay as still as if his death were not feigned.

The cat nudged him.

If he's going to eat me, Pip thought, *why can't he just stop the toying about?*

He'd heard about this horrid game before: the capture, the release, the swatting and batting, the snapping of tiny bones, the near escape just before the final, ripping blow—Pip grew suddenly queasy at the thought.

The mercy of a swift kill was the best he could hope for.

Another touch.

Followed by a poke.

Not sharp claws, but a velvety paw on his side. He eased open an eye. He snapped it shut again at the nearness of the beast.

"Run," the cat whispered. "If the innkeeper sees you, or worse, that monster of a woman I passed on the stair—"

Pip stiffened at the mention of what could only be Croomes the cook.

"What's wrong with you?" the cat hissed. "Why don't you run away?"

This time the tap was not so gentle.

"What's wrong with *me*?" asked Pip, eyes still tightly shut. "I'm behaving as I ought in this situation. What's wrong with *you*?"

"Me? Why, there's nothing—would you get up and leave!" The words were more plea than command.

Pip sat up and blinked curiously at his captor. "You don't want to eat me, then?" This was too incredible. From the moment he'd first seen this animal, the smallest crumbs of understanding had been gathering in his mind, though not quite enough to sate even a mouse's appetite...

He scrabbled to his feet.

This fellow looked like a most regular feline, but otherwise he was all wrong. Pip could feel it. And blast it all, what *was* that smell?

"You...don't...eat...*mice?*" Pip guessed.

"No, I don't," snapped the cat. Failing to disguise the urgency in his voice, he added, "Now would you please run away?"

"You don't eat mice," Pip repeated, rubbing his tiny paws together as he paced back and forth. The puzzle was just too intriguing. And Pip loved puzzles.

"That...is...what...I...said." The cat pronounced each word as if the mouse were hard of hearing.

"But...but why?"

"Because, Crumb Catcher, when I imagine the little claws clutching at my tongue, the rubbery tail thrashing in my throat, I am revolted. Wouldn't you be?"

"I should say so," agreed Pip. "But if you don't eat

mice, why are you here at the Cheshire Cheese, and what do you—?"

There was that distracting odor again.

Could it be?

An outrageous thought plinked into his tiny mind.

Only one way to know with certainty, thought Pip.

He scurried up the nearest shelf.

"Come here," Pip said in his best voice of command, usually reserved for the mouse council.

Imagine a mouse speaking that way to a cat! Skilley ought to have been rightly insulted. But curiosity, which had led to the downfall of so many of his kind, proved the stronger emotion.

"Here I am, then," he said, and presented himself as if for inspection.

"Closer," instructed Pip. He leaned forward until his whiskers brushed against the other's nose. The cat went quite cross-eyed just before he screwed up his face and let out a hearty *ah-choo!*

Nearly blown off his perch, Pip scrambled to regain his balance. Staring at the cat in wonder and confusion, the truth struck him with full force.

"Cheese!" he cried.

CHAPTER SEVEN

Skilley blinked. As the silence between them lengthened, a coldness overtook his heart, then gave way to a prickling warmth. Last came the hot flush of shame.

"Aren't you a clever little mouse," he purred, his voice dangerously sweet.

"I have a name," said Pip, ignoring the menacing tone. He paused to wipe a bit of spittle from his fur.

"What?" Skilley choked back a laugh. A name? How absurd. To most cats, a mouse was a meal—a nauseatingly meaty one to Skilley's way of thinking, but a meal all the same.

"I have a name," repeated the mouse. "It's Pip."

"What kind of a name is that?" Skilley snorted. "Is it short for something?"

"Yes. It's short for Pip. And Pip's me. Don't you have a name?"

Skilley regarded the mouse with interest now. "I could still eat you, you know," he said thoughtfully. Although it was clear from the distaste in his tone, he had no stomach for the words or the mouse.

"Yes, I suppose you could. But I don't think you will—eat me, that is. We both know you don't eat mice. You eat cheese."

"But...but how did you know?"

"I can smell it. It emanates from every pore of you. At first I couldn't place it. So odd to find the scent of cheese lingering on a cat."

"Can others smell it?" Skilley asked with alarm, thinking back to Pinch.

"Hmm. It is rather faint. I'd say you hadn't had much cheese since...Christmas."

Skilley's jaw slackened in amazement. "How could you know that?"

"The mice of Ye Olde Cheshire Cheese have quite a refined sense of smell when it comes to cheese. Don't worry. No sensible mouse among us would object to a cheese-eating cat."

Skilley felt a relief so intense he had to sit, fearful that he might faint. *A cheese-eating cat.* He had never heard those words spoken aloud. Ever. Even by himself.

"Are you all right?" squeaked the mouse.

"I *do* like cheese." The sense of wonder the confession brought was startling. After years of playing the part of the yowling, brawling street cat, Skilley's mask had been stripped away by this insignificant rodent, baring his true self. He had to admit, he had never been entirely cattish.

"Actually, I *love* cheese," he amended.

"Who wouldn't?" piped Pip.

"Don't you think it's...odd?"

"You are speaking to a mouse, you know," said Pip dryly. "What I can't imagine is *not* loving cheese." He rested his paws on his belly and smiled at Skilley. "As to a cat loving cheese? Well, we all have secrets."

The cat flashed him a strange look. "*You?*"

"We're not yet good enough friends for that confidence."

"Friends?" Skilley frowned.

"Certainly. If a person of honorable sensibilities has your darkest secret in his keeping—and asks nothing in return—you might reasonably conclude he is...er, not a foe."

"Honorable sens—?" began Skilley.

"Oh, indeed. Where secrets are concerned, I am a veritable sepulcher."

"Sepul—?"

"Place of perpetual internment," explained Pip.

The cat stared back at him blankly. Pip added helpfully, "Grave. Tomb."

"Then why not just say TOMB?" Skilley's voice rose in exasperation.

"But why say tomb"—Pip went limp and rolled his eyes—"when you can say *seh-pool-kur?*" He drew the word out as if every syllable were made of the finest cheese.

Skilley shook his rattled head. "How did you learn such strange words?"

"That's a tale for another day," said the little mouse. Then he smiled broadly, revealing a prodigious overbite, extraordinary even for a mouse.

This time, Skilley's whiskers twitched with merriment.

"Now," Pip continued, "no more cat-and-mouse games. I know why you've come to Ye Olde Cheshire Cheese. But you'll never get a nibble of its faultless cheese without our help."

"Your help?" Skilley snorted.

"You're a street cat. You don't know about locks and keys," Pip said.

Locks and keys? Pip was wrong. Skilley knew all about those hellish devices, but what they had to do with cheese, he couldn't imagine. "I *don't* understand."

"The cheese is made by Croomes and her sister at a small dairy in Finsbury Park. But it's kept here, in the cellar just beneath us. Being the oldest part of the inn, it's also the coldest. That keeps the cheese delectably fresh."

"What are we waiting for, then?" Skilley made a move toward the stairs. Just as Pip had guessed, he'd had only a few moldy rinds of cheese since Christmas, surviving mostly on back-alley scraps.

"The Cheshire is kept behind a great locked door. Croomes the cook keeps the key. Not that a key would be of any use to us."

"Well, then, how do we get in?" Skilley's voice had taken on an impatient edge.

"We mice have a secret route through stone and mortar—too narrow for you, I'm afraid. As for the door? It opens only when Croomes does the opening."

"I hate doors," muttered Skilley.

"Interesting," said Pip. "Why doors?"

"That is also a tale for another day."

"Fair enough." Pip laughed. "By the way, cat, you never did tell me your name."

"I'm Skilley."

"An honor to meet you, Skilley. Henry will have a mouser. All the better for us if it is a cat that prefers cheese. Might I suggest a bargain then? One that would benefit us all?"

At the word *bargain* Skilley's eyes flashed with inspiration. "Do you mean an exchange of…er…services?"

"Just so. If you will keep us safe, we will reward you each night with the finest cheese in the realm." Pip unleashed one of his matchless smiles.

"I'd have to catch some of you," Skilley warned, all business now.

Pip gave Skilley a hard look. "And release us unharmed, naturally?"

"Are you still suggesting that I might eat you? Ugh. I am strictly a cheese cat."

"Ho! Cat! Where've you got to?" The landlord's voice rumbled down the stairs.

"Now will you run?" Skilley begged.

"Of course." Pip grinned, then leapt onto Skilley's head, scampered down his back, and skittered across the floor. Just before he disappeared through a crack in the wall, he called out the location for a tryst: "Cellar. Midnight. We'll bring the cheese."

"Where?" asked Skilley.

"The cellar! Just follow your nose!" Then Pip vanished.

When the landlord spied Skilley licking his lips in anticipation of the finest cheese in England, he said, "Tasty was he? Well, my fine mouser, there's plenty more where that one came from."

thimblejigger

milch

balamy

whiddler

toff

snilch

hookem-snivey

I culled these fantastical words this morning as I stood on the corner near the Café Royal and listened to the street sellers and patterers. I jotted these down quickly, lest they slip from my memory.

Also worth noting: the Cheshire Cheese cat has caught my fancy. He is a handsome blue with a most comical tail. He appears so very coarse. But the writer in me imagines there is more to this fellow than scars and swagger. Is he a brute? He certainly appears as one—then so does Sydney Carton, the hero of my current story.

Four sleepless nights, and I have no opening line.

I haven't jumped in the Thames yet.

Still, it is only Tuesday.

CHAPTER EIGHT

They will never be persuaded to trust a cat, thought Pip. *Not after what happened to Maldwyn.*

The mouse citizenry of Ye Olde Cheshire Cheese was assembling in the musty attic. Pip was perched atop a wooden dressmaker's form in a corner of the room, surveying the scene before him. Only a quarter of an hour had passed since he had issued the signal: a flicker of the gaslight.

Twice.

It was an old code, devised by some long-forgotten foremouse. One flicker called the mouse council to convene; two signaled every able-bodied mouse to an urgent general assembly. Three flickers—well, thank Providence, that extreme measure had never in his memory been called for.

The mice had come in response to Pip's call, scurrying up drainpipes, climbing dumbwaiter ropes, and navigating the old familiar paths behind plaster walls.

Now the attic seemed almost alive, every surface rippling with movement. Mirrors and chests and lamps and bellows vanished beneath a quivering, undulating blanket of restless mice.

Thousands of mice.

All crowded into a space fit for a quarter of their number. Even the two gaslight fixtures held a hundred or so of the younger, more acrobatic mice.

Pip licked his paw...

wiped his nose...

licked his paw...

In Pip's lifetime there had been but one other such gathering. It, too, had been over the issue of an uninvited guest. Pip brushed those thoughts aside. For better or worse, that matter was settled. He had a more pressing problem at present.

Pip noted the last of the stragglers as they slipped in through a hole in the ceiling.

It was time to call the meeting to order. He extended his front paw. In his palm he held a morsel of cheese as radiant as a nugget of Spanish gold. In a slow, sweeping gesture he presented it to the room of wiggling, wriggling mice—and within moments he was looking out at nearly ten thousand pair of spellbound eyes.

In for a penny, in for a pound, thought Pip.

He took as deep a breath as mouse lungs would permit and began: "My esteemed friends and neighbors, today we have been afforded by the hard hand of Fate…a gentle blow. A cat has come to The Cheese—"

A high-pitched murmur ran through the crowd.

"Silence, please!"

Again Pip held aloft the bit of Cheshire. A slow lulling of the chatter was followed by a tense stillness. "I say a *gentle* blow, for it seems that where we should expect enmity, we have found amity; where we might rightly expect a threat, we have found goodwill. This is no ordinary cat. This cat has no taste for mice. He eats…" Pip paused for effect. "He eats CHEESE."

It is not, sadly, within the God-given talents of this writer to describe the scene that unfolded. Imagine, if you will, a House of Commons composed of ten thousand diminutive members of parliament—all squeaking and thrashing their tails in alarm, disbelief, and dissent.

CHAPTER NINE

The hidden creature observed the mice with a growing sense of horror. A cat at Ye Olde Cheshire Cheese?

Folly.

Worse than folly.

Catastrophe.

His good eye flitted back and forth, trying to take in the chaos through the narrow chink in the plaster. His damaged eye blinked and refused to participate.

An abandoned garret, tucked behind another newer attic, had been his sanctuary and his prison these nine weary months. Certainly, his keepers' attempts at providing him with small comforts such as fresh straw and scraps of suet had been welcomed, but Ye Olde Cheshire Cheese remained to his sensibilities (and he had many) as sure a prison as Newgate.

Tonight, he grudgingly admitted to himself, the room's isolation had been to his advantage. It had allowed him to observe and listen with growing horror to the disastrous proposal that was being put to a vote—just on the other side of that plaster wall.

He could hardly contain his dismay and outrage. Had they forgotten that England's very survival hung in the balance? If they had only asked him—well, he knew why they hadn't asked him. He'd have put an immediate stop to any talk of striking a bargain with a…cat.

Cat.

Even the word was distasteful to him. It was a small, mean word, one that began harshly and ended crossly.

And this creature knew about cats. He winced at the ache in his shoulder, more memory now than pain. Yet never had he felt the consequences of his rash choices more keenly.

It was then that he allowed regret to give way to a stronger, more pressing feeling: an overwhelming sense of duty. Her Majesty the Queen, he was certain, must be mad with worry at his absence…and all that it implied.

He must reach the Tower.

But how?

CHAPTER TEN

Ye Olde Cheshire Cheese! Within its walls Skilley
discovered a wondrous warren of

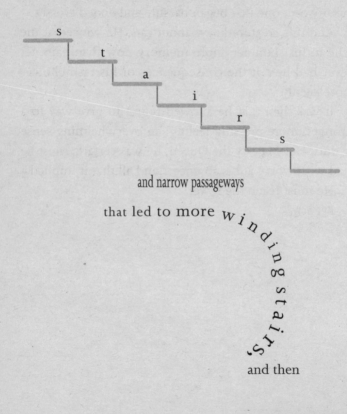

s
    t
        a
            i
                r
                    s

and narrow passageways

that led to more winding stairs,

and then

up

to hallways that abruptly ended,

or if not,

led

d
o
w
n

to even more twisting,
sometimes crooked
sTaIrS that
finally tumbled
into dining rooms or

char-rooms or

dungeonlike cellars.

At the center of it all brooded Croomes, the cook.

A culinary tyrant, she ruled the nether regions of the inn with an iron ladle.

Her copper pots and saucepans
    bubbled
        and boiled
            and steamed
                and frothed
with the constant cooking of brews and hearty dishes. And through every brick and timber of Croomes's domain there lingered the sweet smell of history, along with the musty odor of yesteryear's Yorkshire pudding, roast lamb, mutton chops, and steak and kidney pie.

Skilley had found the kitchen.

And what was this? A swinging door? As if ordinary doors weren't dangerous enough.

Croomes the cook

It took perfect timing to pass through unharmed. On the other side, the smells melded into an enticing confusion of the savory and the sweet. And oh, the clanking and clanging! To Skilley's ears they were like bells that hammered out a song to gaiety and...food, food, food!

He slipped behind a great basket of onions where he could watch the splendid scene before him. It appeared to have been staged by some great gastronomic genius.

Cooking fires leapt and crackled, serving girls swept in and out with a creak and pop of the swinging door, and potboys laden with foaming mugs of ale ducked and swerved and scurried about, laughing and bawling out orders to one another.

Skilley's head bobbed in time to the rhythm. It was a symphony of—

"What the bony blazes is that beast doing in me kitchen?"

CHAPTER ELEVEN

The silence was instant and absolute.

Even the fires shrank back from the horrific voice that boomed from a mouth—no, a gaping maw—that could have swallowed Admiral Lord Nelson's fleet in a single gulp.

Skilley would have laughed at the amusing scene of a boy caught in mid-bustle, his foot raised in the air, but for the monstrous shape that trundled toward that boy.

Croomes advanced on him, her forehead prismatic with sweat and grease.

Skilley had seen her just once before: a formidable figure of a woman, betwixt square and round, who was nearly as wide as she was tall. Her meaty hand pointed a wooden spoon at Skilley. But only for an instant. Immediately the spoon whipped about and cracked the kitchen boy on top of his head.

"Get that flea-infested ankle-scratcher out of here!"

The boy dropped to the floor, then scrambled out of reach.

"That cat!" growled the woman. "Get it—"

She was interrupted by a spewing, spitting pot on the stove behind her. "Oh, calamity!" she wailed. "Me fricassee!"

The spell was broken. The kitchen dance resumed. The cook spun about to rescue her sauce. As she did, the iron ring tied to her apron strings came loose and flew across the room.

The ring of keys rattled to a stop at Skilley's feet.

Notable among them was a brass key. It was larger than the rest, vastly older, and worn to a dull sheen.

What luck! Skilley suspected he knew which lock that key would open. Wouldn't Pip be surprised? Not that he cared about impressing a mouse, mind.

"Ach! Burnt to a clinker!"

Skilley glanced up. The cook glowered at the spoon of sauce she had just tasted.

"Ruint! Throw it out! Start afresh, you blundering nancy-mongers!!"

While Croomes was thus distracted, Skilley nosed at the key ring. He nudged it up and clasped it between his teeth. As stealthy as ever a cat could be, he turned to the door, but then had to skitter back as it swung wide.

At that very instant, a bloodcurdling cry erupted from behind him. "ME KEYS!"

There never was such a free-for-all of boys and scullery maids, leaping and hurling themselves out of the cook's thundering path.

As Croomes approached, a lightning thought jolted Skilley into action.

Rather than cower, he high-stepped boldly to the center of the room, never taking his eyes off the raging cook. The unfortunate potboy she had just captured tugged on her sleeve and pointed at the cat with one hand while protecting his head with the other.

The look the woman shot at Skilley would have stopped the Angel of Death in its tracks, yet Skilley resolutely continued his approach. With all eyes upon him, he placed the key ring on the toe of her colossal boot.

As instantly as it had appeared, the red-faced frown was supplanted by a more frightening look.

It would be criminal to call it a smile.

And yet a smile it was.

There was no other word to describe it: the widespread lips, the tea-stained teeth, and the bunched-up cheeks that looked like two overripe pomegranates.

"Brought back me keys, have you?" Croomes cooed. Her crooning, sweet as treacle, was even more unsettling than her smile.

She bent down to snatch up the keys with one hand. With the other, she gently chucked Skilley under the chin. "What a wonderful puss!" Then she leaned closer and inhaled deeply. With a disquieting gaze into his eyes, she whispered, "You're an odd one, then." She sighed, as if in resignation. "Very well, I wager there be enough mice for us both."

With a pat on his head that nearly sent him sprawling to the flagstones, she held up the iron ring. Her sausage finger stabbed the air for emphasis as she declared, "Take a lesson in respect from this kitty, the rest of you scallirascals!"

Skilley jutted out his chin and strolled proudly out of the kitchen, timing his exit to coincide with a wide swing of the door.

Once on the other side, he nearly collapsed from fright. The moment he regained his composure, he firmly resolved to avoid Croomes as much as possible in future.

CHAPTER TWELVE

Midnight loomed.

Skilley slipped past the still busy kitchen and down the dark stairs. As he neared the vaulted cellar, he breathed in the peculiar, almost fungal odor of old bricks, wood, and dirt. At the bottom of the staircase, a soft light drifted through the entryway. He stepped into a room of arched ceilings and age-old stones. So this was the oldest part of the inn? Lying about were wine casks, tinned meats, and sacks of grain. And beyond them stood a heavy, pockmarked door, crafted in another age. Could this be where Croomes hoarded her famous cheese?

Skilley released a shudder.

Doors.

He settled in a corner to wait. He was half an hour early to his appointment.

How did he know it to be half past eleven? It is a fact that all intelligent animals (except for those poor, distractible humans) have an unerring sense of time. They need no Roman numeral on an enameled clock face, no shadow on a sundial—no slices of hours, slivers of minutes, splinters of seconds—to inform them of a mystery carried deep within.

Animals carry time in their bones.

So it was that Skilley had no need of a pocket watch to assure him that he had arrived early. All day he'd fought a craving for cheese that threatened to consume him. But as the minutes passed, the cat began to wonder if he had been taken for a fool—

"Ahem!" squeaked a small voice, demanding Skilley's immediate attention.

Pip was there at last.

"You came!" Skilley's surprise was evident.

"Of course, I came. I'm a mouse of my word."

Skilley peered past him, scanning the cellar for the bargained cheese.

From behind his back Pip produced a fragrant yellow morsel. Holding it in his cupped paws, he presented it to the cat with great ceremony.

"To seal our bargain," he explained.

"Er, uh, yes…," Skilley dithered.

"You seem disappointed," said Pip.

"Well, no. Not really." He sniffed at the crumb. "It is Cheshire cheese after all."

"Of the red variety. Hence its magnificent golden hue. And," Pip added, his furry chest swelling with pride, "the finest in England."

"Thank you," Skilley said. He would have to rethink this arrangement. Surely, they couldn't expect him to live on—

"No. Thank you." Pip cleared his throat as he gestured toward the shadows of the far corner. "Pssssssst. Come now."

The cat and mouse waited. A full twenty seconds they waited. There was no response. Pip glanced apologetically back at Skilley. "If you'll pardon me for just a moment. They're in need of a bit of coaxing, I'm afraid." He vanished into the stygian darkness.

Skilley strained his ears at the frantic whispers.

"He's still a C-C-C-CAT!" blurted one voice.

More murmurs. At last Pip reappeared.

"My humble apologies," he said. He then turned and addressed the shadows, this time with impatience. "Look sharp now! We have an agreement!"

Skilley stared into the gloom, trying to make out who—or what—was hidden within it.

Then a mouse (much smaller and younger than Pip) edged out of the darkness. In her paws she clutched a bit of cheese the size of a pea; for her small person, this was a great burden. As she left the meager offering, she paused and stared up at the cat, an act which sent her nearly toppling over backward. Righting herself, she scuttled in retreat to hide behind Pip.

Two pieces of cheese: enough to content a mouse, but hardly enough to tempt a cat. Ah, well. Skilley wondered whether it would be rude to eat them both now (the cheese bits, not the mice) or to save a snack for—

But wait.

A creaky old rodent with notched ears appeared. His whiskers hung like a mossy beard from his chin. A spent wooden matchstick supported his every arthritic step. He dropped the third bit of cheese, then nudged it with his stick so that it rolled unevenly toward Skilley. With a sideways tilt to his head, the old mouse gathered up his tail and, displaying great dignity, hobbled back to Pip.

Two more mice scampered from the darkness, followed by three, four, five more, each with an offering in his arms. Soon, an unending queue of cheese-bearing mice snaked from the shadows, until a golden mountain of Cheshire rose before Skilley.

Even then, the advancing line, now composed mostly of the curious, continued. Few of the mice had ever seen a cat. None had ever been this close to one and lived, and yet, in a matter of moments, Skilley had gained their confidence.

But it's not me, he thought. *It's Pip they trust.*

"Thank you," he said to Pip, and this time he meant it.

"D-d-does it bite?" piped the littlest mouse.

"He chews," Pip said. "But only cheese."

"And an occasional herring, when the fishmonger's eye wanders," Skilley added with a wink at the small one, who ducked behind Pip again.

The oldest mouse hitched himself forward. "We appreciate your alliance with us, despite your unfortunate ancestry. Just keep away from Maldwyn and you'll be—"

"Hush!" cried a chorus of voices.

With a stricken look, the old fellow clamped a paw over his mouth.

"Who's Maldwyn?" Skilley asked.

The codger waggled his walking stick at the cat. "Someone it would do well for you to avoid."

Skilley's glance slid toward Pip. "Who's Maldwyn?" he insisted.

Pip shook his head. "That information is not part of our agreement."

"But how do I avoid this Maldwyn if—"

He was interrupted by a tug on his fur. The brave little girl-mouse, no bigger than a walnut, stepped back and clasped her paws before her. In a singsong voice, she recited a verse:

> It is in truth a well-known fact,
> That curiosity killed the cat.

Skilley threw back his head and laughed at her impudence. When he regained control, he bent down and touched his nose to hers. "Ah, but satisfaction brought him back!"

In response, the tiny mouse gave a squeal. To his horror she flung herself onto his snout, took him firmly by the whiskers, and planted a small kiss on the tip of his nose.

"Too!" Her father, who was by nature a somewhat nervous mouse, rushed toward her. He was as taken aback by this display as was the cat.

As he tried to pull her away, she lifted her head and chirped, "Oh, Papa, Too likes the cat. He smells like us!"

"Too?" Skilley turned to Pip for an answer.

"Too," Pip said with a grin, "is her name. As in 'too loud, too curious, too impulsive.' If one can be too much of anything, that's Too."

The company of mice responded with hoots and good-natured tittering.

Too's embarrassed father shrugged, then swept her up onto his shoulders. Hugging his neck, she rested her chin between her papa's ears and smiled up at Skilley.

CHAPTER THIRTEEN

Purest heaven. That's what it was.

Cheese aged to perfection. Cheshire with just the perfect tang, the perfect roundness of flavor, the perfect tussle between smooth and crumbly.

Yes, it was unquestionable.

This was indeed the finest cheese in London.

And Skilley should know. Hadn't he been born behind the stove of a workhouse kitchen? Hadn't his first memories been of curds and whey and cheese? And hadn't he thieved cheeses from every milkman and greengrocer once he'd been tossed onto the streets to—?

No. He wouldn't think of that now.

He let each bite linger on his tongue until he could no longer resist taking another. The pile dwindled as his admiration grew.

Pip watched in fascination. "Marvelous, isn't it?" he inquired.

"Mmm." Skilley thought back to a word he'd once heard a fine lady use when staring through a millinery shop window. The object of her devotion was a hat, all feathers and ribbons.

Wanting to show Pip that even a street cat could pick up a fancy word or two, he whispered, "Dee-vine," and his eyes rolled back in rapture.

"Divine. Now, that's a fine word," said Pip. "See, you do know some wonderful words."

Skilley remembered the gentleman who had accompanied the lady. *Now what was it he had called the hat? He had used the word with great force. Ah, yes.*

"Preee-posterous!" he cried.

"I quite understand and agree," said Pip with a laugh. "Preposterous cheese, indeed."

"Have a bite," Skilley offered.

"No, no. I—well, perhaps just a crumb... Oh, but I must resist. It is, after all, yours."

The moment was historic: a cat and a mouse with a mutual love of cheese. And although the strangeness of the moment wasn't lost on either Pip or Skilley, and although each stole curious glances at the other, neither remarked on it.

That fact alone was worthy of note.

CHAPTER FOURTEEN

That night, Adele the barmaid set out a flowered cushion behind the bar for Skilley.

Henry scoffed at the gesture. "That old tomcat doesn't need such foofery," he declared.

"I says 'e does," she shot back. "Anythin' what'll rid us of them vermin..." She pushed a wisp of hair from her forehead. "Well, all I says is give 'im 'is due."

More interested in currying Henry's favor, Skilley sniffed at the cushion and curled his lip in disdain. He chose instead a particularly drafty corner, wherein he defiantly settled himself.

"See," said Henry, "a right hardy kitty, to be sure."

But once the inn had closed for the night, the last customer had been ushered out the door, and the lights dimmed to nothing; once Adele had patted the cat good night and the landlord had shuffled upstairs to his own bed, Skilley left the cheerless corner and curled up on the cushion behind the bar. He sighed as he nestled into its floral comfort.

A safe place, a full belly, and a warm bed.

His mind relaxed with the overwhelming sense of ease. He was well on his way to a sweeter slumber than he had ever known when a clatter echoed through the darkness. There followed a distant scratching and scraping noise.

He struggled to open his eyes. "Don't those mice ever sleep?" he mumbled to himself.

Then he rolled onto his back and sighed again, only to be disturbed once more, this time by a thump and a bump. And a faraway rattle. Noises that seemed a touch too large for his new-found allies. Noises that came from far above—from the very rooftop. *Rats?* he surmised. Then a strange, inhuman cry set the very tips of Skilley's ears to tingling. He was on his feet and halfway up the stairs to investigate before his common sense took hold. *Don't be a fool*, he told himself. *Go back to bed. Tomorrow you—*

Another hideous cry struck his eardrums.

And a crash.

He raced up the stairs, unwilling to be surprised later in his bed by whatever dread thing might haunt those upper regions of the inn.

At the top of the attic steps he stopped, jerked to a halt by the silhouette of a human figure in the corner gloom. He slunk behind a hatbox, wishing now he had stayed in bed. He sniffed at the air, but the only odors he detected were those of mice and dust and something he didn't recognize—something not human, not cat, not mouse. Something decaying…

His tail twitched with nerves. The human shape in the corner remained still. Had Skilley recognized it as a woman's dress form, he would have been mightily embarrassed at his suspicions.

A sharp bang from behind the nearest wall almost separated Skilley from his hide. He was surprised by his own alacrity, as, in a flash, he tore back down the several flights of stairs. Within moments, he found himself beneath the floral cushion. And there he remained for some hours, comforted only by the steady *ka-thump ka-thump* of his heart.

Sleep did, at last, come to Skilley. He slept well past sunrise, not stirring even when the first faint rustlings from the rooms above announced that the humans were on the move.

He awoke only for a moment when Henry trudged into the chop room, still in his nightshirt and half-open dressing gown—a disturbing sight that caused Skilley to bury his head deeper beneath the cushion. From there he could just hear the landlord's muttered words, "Curséd ghost! Why my tavern? Why not The Old Bell? Couldn't sleep a wink all night. How about you, cat? Sleeping now, are you? Well, rest up. Good day for mousing."

Skilley did not budge. He even ignored the breakfast rasher of bacon that Adele placed before him. He slept, though fitfully, through the morning deliveries.

It was the volley of bone-rattling screams that finally roused him to the day.

Henry

CHAPTER FIFTEEN

"What's all the blunderbuss?"

The thundering voice of Croomes as she approached the dining room momentarily drowned out Adele's shrill cries. In response to the wailing, the cook had set aside a bowl of rising bread dough, ready for kneading. She was not in a charitable mood.

She might have trampled Skilley as she charged into the room—had he not deftly shot past her to find refuge under one of the chairs.

Croomes stopped cold when she saw the barmaid. Adele's wild hair and ashen face looked the very portrait of terror.

"Th-th-there! It c-c-come at me! It…it…it was 'orrible." Adele spoke the words in telegraphic hiccups as she pointed toward the cone of sugar standing on the sideboard.

Seeing her tremble, knees-to-chin on the tavern counter, one would never have guessed this was the same girl who had tongue-lashed the coal man that very morning for trying to cheat her out of a half-sack of coal.

The indignant man had stormed off—but not before correcting the shortage and leaving Adele with a handful of coins and a coy smile on her face. But that had been hours earlier.

"Wicked mouses," the girl whimpered from her precarious perch. She drew her feet up beneath her. "Why me? Why don't no one else see 'em? I kin 'ardly cut into a slab of cheese without settin' me eyes on one."

It was true. Adele seemed to have an uncommon gift for uncovering mice: reach into a sack of flour, sweep behind a dustbin, overturn a teacup, and there one would be, staring back at her with shiny black eyes.

(If only she'd known how popular a game Tormenting Adele had become with the inn's younger mice.)

She shivered again as Croomes rolled her eyes and shoved past her. The cook headed for the sideboard, leading with her cleaver.

"I'm here, ain't I?" she bellowed. "Stop your miserable caterwauling!"

A frantic Pip stood on his hind legs and pressed his furry belly against the hard, sandy surface of the sugar cone. He negotiated a firm hold on the sheltered side, his breath sounding dreadfully loud to his own ears.

There's no way out of this one, Pip, old fellow.

Adele had been a surprise, but a manageable one. In Pip's mind, she was among those harmless souls who could be depended on to deliver splendid shrieks at the first glimpse of a mouse: her punctuated screams, spaced precisely two seconds apart, were as reliable as the trains at Paddington Station. Despite this, Pip didn't mind Adele. She held no true threat. And like most girls, she reminded him of Nell.

Poor Nell.

Pip was brought back from his reverie by the snorting and snuffling of Croomes. This was followed by the groaning of the floorboards as she drew cautiously nearer with each step.

Had Adele given him away? Had she pointed out the sugar cone?

Steady, Pip.

He could smell her now.

Black pudding.

The licorice scent of fennel seeds.

Sweat.

Her shadow fell across the surface of the board, a hand took hold of the top of the sugar cone, and Pip was lifted above Croomes's head as she searched all about.

"What is it I'm looking for, girl?"

"I told ya. A rat!" Adele spat the word.

"And why are you calling me from me kitchen when you should be calling for the cat?"

At that crucial moment, Skilley appeared on the scene. Quick-thinking as ever, he let out a yowl, then leapt at Croomes's hand, knocking the sugar cone— and the mouse still clinging to it—to the ground.

"Blast and blatherbait!" Croomes cried as she inspected the small drops of blood beading up around her knuckles. Then she spied Pip in a motionless gray heap next to the baseboard, the sugar cone shattered all about him. Croomes's response was unexpected.

She laughed.

"A mouse? You had me forsake me loaves for a mouse? I thought you said you saw a rat?"

"They's all the same, ain't they? Filthy vermin!"

"They're not the same, not by halves! A mouse is nothing like a rat."

As the two distracted women argued, Skilley snatched up Pip in his mouth.

"Afraid of a little mouse," Croomes muttered in disgust, wagging her enormous head as she turned to leave. "Best get used to 'em if you're working at The Cheese."

Adele descended awkwardly from the countertop and fished about for her lost shoe. To the cook's retreating wardrobe of a back she shot, "Shows what she knows."

Her next comment was directed at Skilley. "What we're in need of is reinforcements. Two mouse catchers is bound to be better than one, eh?"

Skilley would have gulped but for the contents of his mouth.

Croomes, who had paused in the doorway to pin up a loose strand of graying hair, heard every word and felt a lurch of panic. One cat had not greatly worried her, but two?

A most curious thing.

Our Cheshire Cheese cat is a mouser of formidable abilities. Not an hour passes but he parades by with a new victim in his jaws. Or does he? Either I have lost the keen edge to my powers of observation, or it is ever the same fellow being caught over and over again: a small gray mouse with the most singular front teeth.

Thus, either I am gone mad, or this cat is catching and releasing the same mouse.

But why? Now, there's a story that begs writing!

As to my own worries, I still have no opening lines for my own tale of revolution and redemption.

Aha! The blue has just sprinted past the chop room with another mouse in his jaws. This little intrigue has me quite distracted—

CHAPTER SIXTEEN

Skilley didn't stop until he reached the top landing, the one that led to the garret in the older part of the attic. Gently, he loosened his jaw and deposited Pip atop a stack of old newspapers.

"This is going to cost extra, you know," Skilley said.

A prone Pip exhaled a long breath that made his whiskers rise and fall. Triumphantly, he held up the nip of sugar he'd managed to hold onto during the encounter with Croomes.

Still in one piece.

Excellent.

"I rescued you from that madwoman so you could have a nip of sugar? I thought you only ate cheese—" Skilley stopped cold. It couldn't be. Or could it? Within moments he was laughing so earnestly that he had to lean against the pile of papers in order to steady himself.

"I believe I've stumbled on your secret, Pip."

The mouse sat up, alert.

Skilley directed a knowing look at the nip of sugar in his companion's paw. "Come to think of it, I've yet to see you eat cheese."

"What are you getting at?"

"I don't eat mice, and you don't eat cheese!"

Once again hilarity got the better of him and Skilley collapsed against the carelessly piled newsprint.

This time the tower toppled, taking Pip with it.

As the papers washed across the floor in a tidal wave of London news and advertisements, Pip nimbly rode a front page as far as the opposite wall before the impact sent him sprawling.

Skilley slumped to the floorboards, overcome with laughter.

Pip was not nearly so amused. Scrambling to his feet, he responded to the accusation. "I'll have you know I adore cheese! The sugar is for Mald—"

Their eyes met and locked. For one long, uneasy moment neither looked away…nor spoke. Skilley sighed, then padded over to Pip.

"Whatever scheme you have going, all this secrecy and hugger-mugger is wearing a little thin, my friend. Is there a limit to how many times I must save your life before you'll come to trust me?"

He stopped when he saw the stricken look on Pip's face. "What's wrong?"

Pip was no longer looking at Skilley. He was staring down at the inky smudges on the paper beneath him.

What followed was even more baffling to Skilley. The little rodent pressed his nose to the paper and began to travel back and forth down the page in a most methodical way, never once lifting his eyes from the black markings. When at last he stopped, all that was left of the morsel of sugar was a silty trail along the paper; in his distress, Pip had crushed it entirely. So shaken did he appear that Skilley was fearful for his well-being.

"Pip?" he whispered.

The mouse turned to him, as though in a trance. "Maldwyn. He was telling the truth." Without further explanation, Pip darted into the nearest mouse hole.

"Got away again, did he?" It was the pipe-organ voice that had introduced Skilley into the inn. Mr. Dickens, wasn't it?

Skilley shot the man a look of singular indifference. Dickens leaned against the stairway banister, crossed his arms, and met the cat's glance with a questioning gaze of his own. Skilley intensified his glare. The writer tried to match it, but staring down a cat is a difficult sport.

"Very well," chuckled Dickens, backing away. "But I will say, that mouse of yours seems to have more lives than you, my good cat."

CHAPTER SEVENTEEN

Skilley watched Dickens retreat down the stairs and listened as the man's footfalls grew fainter and fainter. His first instincts had been on the mark; this human wanted watching.

But now there lay a more tantalizing task at hand.

What had Pip discovered in those fish wrappings to alarm him so? Skilley padded 'round the newspapers and tried to make sense of what he saw. And what did the shadowy Maldwyn have to do with any of it?

Skilley studied the newspapers that had spilled across the floor. No matter how many times he walked around them, they remained what they had always been: fish wrappings. So why had Pip—

Thunk! Thud! Skattle! Crash!

Then silence.

Skilley slowly raised his eyes toward the ceiling.

CHAPTER EIGHTEEN

Maldwyn paced restlessly, his tottering steps as jerky as a marionette's.

The room was wrecked.

"You look, er, unwell," Pip said tactfully, scratching at an ear.

Indeed, in the dim light, Maldwyn appeared to be multipally afflicted with palsy, gout, dropsy, and possibly—judging by the hacks and wheezes—a touch of ague.

"If there is anything we can do to make you more comfortable, sir…," Pip began. He silently cursed himself for having destroyed that hard-won bit of sugar; even Maldwyn sweetened considerably after consuming a lump or two.

"That won't be necessary. You have all done quite enough." The words were pleasant, the tone glacial.

Pip could stand it no longer. "You were telling the truth, sir! I see that now!" Those two brief lines, explosively uttered, left him breathless. He looked at Maldwyn in abject misery.

Maldwyn turned his best eye toward the mouse and gave what passed for a shrug, as though this obvious truth was of little matter now.

He resumed his pacing; his bobbing shadow was made all the more eerie by the single guttering candle with its sooty tendrils of smoke.

"Dear, dear," Pip mumbled. This was going badly.

He licked his paw...

flicked his ear...

licked his paw.

Why had he been so unwilling to believe Maldwyn's claims?

When Nell had first brought Maldwyn to the garret and her mouse friends, no one had expected him to live out the day. The rare times he'd spoken, his claims had been so ridiculous they'd believed him to be hallucinating, or senile, or worse yet—barking mad.

Despite their misgivings, the mice tended to him for Nell's sake. And then, he'd improved. Quite miraculously, and, some thought, in poor taste.

The more he recovered, the more outrageous his stories became. They were, of course, great fun for the younger mice. The little ones crowded around his sickbed, a dozen at a time, to hear just one more, until their mothers appeared, tsk-tsking and nudging them off to their nests. Soon, however, his insistence on the truth of the tales grew dangerous.

It was Old Bodkin's turn at the night watch when Maldwyn saw his chance. Purposefully choosing his longest, dullest story, he droned on until the elderly mouse—struggling to stay  awake—tucked his paws under his beard for warmth and fell into a deep sleep.

Bodkin was still snoring when Maldwyn slipped out to the landing, and nearly awakened the household with his cry: "I demand to see Her Majesty!"

Thanks be, the landlord was a determined sleeper. Nell reached Maldwyn first. With a combination of flattery and gentle firmness, she convinced him to return to his hiding place before he roused every soul in the place.

Still, Nell wouldn't hear of turning him out.

And the mouse council had given in, although it was decided, quite prudently, to confine Nell's "guest" to his quarters—much to Maldwyn's dismay.

Squaraaaank.

The loud squeak of a floorboard brought Pip back to the present. It would be hard to say who was more startled, he or Maldwyn, as they both turned to stare at the intruder.

"Skilley?" said Pip.

The cat stared back with an equal measure of shock. As he looked from Pip to his companion, Skilley stammered, "M-M-Maldwyn is...a *crow?*"

Pip shook his head furiously at the cat, but Skilley failed to appreciate the enormity of his blunder.

Maldwyn took a step toward Skilley. Drawing up to his full height, which was impressive, he spoke with profound dignity: "I am no crow, sir. Neither am I rook, nor magpie, nor jackdaw, nor grackle, nor blackbird."

"He's a *raven*," Pip hissed at Skilley. Maldwyn silenced the mouse with a horrific caw. Then he pinned Skilley with a wintry stare and declared himself with an elegance that removed any doubt of his lineage.

"I am of the House of Battenberg: a Raven of the Tower of London, property of Queen Victoria of England. As I stand or fall, *so does the Empire!*"

CHAPTER NINETEEN

"So you're the ghost in the garret!"

Skilley's remark was not well received.

And when the cry came from deep within the raven's throat—a chilling sound somewhere between a squawk and a screech—the fur along Skilley's back rose to attention.

"Calm yourself, sir!" Pip rushed to Maldwyn's side.

"He's a cat!" Maldwyn snapped at Pip, as if this fact might have gone unnoticed by the young mouse.

"He is a cat," Pip consented, his voice calm despite the crackling tension in the room. "But, upon my word, he is a most unusual cat. He does not eat mice—Skilley prefers cheese. You must agree, that quality alone makes him most uncatlike. No doubt you already know this, having observed our meeting through your peephole…"

Pip paused to lick his paw…

to stroke his chin…

"The cat." The raven recalled Pip to the issue at hand.

"The cat," interrupted Skilley, "can speak for himself."

Pip released a moan.

Skilley ignored him and directed his comments to Maldwyn. "Admittedly, I know little of Tower ravens, but aren't they generally found in the Tower? I would dearly love to hear how one came to be hidden here, in the attic of the Cheshire Cheese."

"Tell him, Maldwyn," Pip encouraged. "He'll help us. I know he will. You will, won't you, Skilley?" Pip's smile held nothing back.

"That depends. The only thing I enjoy better than a good cheese is a good story," said Skilley, settling down before the raven.

It was up to Maldwyn to take up the challenge.

Or not.

CHAPTER TWENTY

Maldwyn had told the tale before, most often to young ravens in need of their history lessons. He had never expected to be called upon to tell it to a cat. His eye fell first on Pip, then washed over Skilley in a perfunctory fashion.

With a warning clack of his beak and a clearing of his throat, he began his story:

There have always been ravens on the White Hill—

"The White Hill?" Skilley asked.

"The Tower of London sits on the White Hill. No interruptions!"

Skilley grunted and Maldwyn began anew.

There have always been ravens on the White Hill.
Before our beloved Queen Victoria.
Before the madness of King George.
Before the golden age of Queen Elizabeth.
We were there.

Our destiny became fixed in the days of the giant king, Bran the Blessed. The king was killed in battle defending Britain, and upon his death Bran's own men cut off his head.

"Spare me the moans of disgust," the raven squawked at Skilley. "Merciful heavens! I had no idea cats could be so squeamish. As I said, they cut off his head. Now, may I continue my history?"

Pip and Skilley glanced at each other before nodding at the raven.

"Where was I then...?" Maldwyn fluttered one wing, then settled again on his perch. "Oh yes. The head."

It was believed, in those times, that a man's head housed his soul and would cry out in warning if enemies neared.

King Bran's men buried his skull on the White Hill—a place, remember, where ravens had always dwelled—and they made certain it was facing France to guard against invasion.

There Bran has remained, forever watchful.

And there we ravens have remained. Living tombstones, we guard the great king. He guards England. For centuries it was understood that if we were left to our duty, our land would be safe from intruders.

Then came Charles II, the Merry Monarch.

Maldwyn paused and let out a hoarse laugh. "Merry Monarch? Bah! Brainless buffoon, I would say. Even Bran's decayed skull were not so empty as that. But his wasn't the only such mind in the court." The raven's jet black eye flitted from Skilley to Pip; certain of their attention, he continued.

Alas, King Charles had more love for the distant stars than he had for day-to-day matters in his own court. It was he who established a Royal Observatory in the White Tower. All went well until his astronomer—an even greater idiot, by the name of John Flamsteed—objected to what he called the "infestation" of ravens.

Enraged, the raven turned to his listeners. "Imagine, will you? The audacity to call our presence an infestation! Yes, well…" Maldwyn made a visible effort to calm himself and returned to his tale.

Charles responded to his astronomer's whimpering complaints by ordering every last bird butchered.

Pip couldn't hold back a squeaky gasp, and Skilley's ears flattened against his skull.

"As I live and breathe," said the raven. "I swear it to be true. But do not worry your heads yet."

Before the order could be carried out, a snowy-haired soothsayer appeared unbidden to the king. His name is lost to history, but not his pluck. He predicted the direst of consequences for the kingdom, and merry old Charles himself, if a single raven were harmed.

This time the raven interrupted his own story. Apparently, the wicked tidbit was too delicious to be resisted.

"It is said that the old fortune-teller so frightened dear Charles that the king soiled his knickers—a great embarrassment to most humans, I understand." He chuckled to himself. "An undignified tale, perhaps, yet it somehow comforts me to believe it." He picked up the thread of the story again, trying to regain his composure.

In any event, the king swore an oath that there would always be ravens in the White Tower—never fewer than six—so long as he ruled England.

From that day, each monarch has accepted our presence with everything from indulgence to indifference to grudging respect.

And England has been, for the most part, spared great harm. That is until I, on that ill-fated evening, made a most unwise decision. There were six ravens in the Tower until that day.

Now there are only five.

CHAPTER TWENTY-ONE

For a long while, Maldwyn seemed lost in thought.

"Five?" asked Skilley, finally daring to break the silence. "What happened to the—"

Pip gave a little cough and rolled his eyes as he nodded toward the raven.

Maldwyn dropped his head and spoke as if from a dream. "I remember the moment clearly. It was a most unusual day for London. The clouds, thin and gauzy, stretched overhead like bits of cheesecloth; the sky was a tantalizing blue. I now believe I was bewitched by the dazzling beauty of that sky.

"Then there was the business of my wings. Because of my age and faithful service, the Ravenmaster had chosen to let my clipped wings regrow.

"But I betrayed him. Such is the lure of spring, even on the old.

"I am the eldest of all the ravens, yet I was a mere fledgling when I last knew the joy of flight. I thought only to soar across the river and back. But once I caught the draft of warm air rising from the Thames, all my reason fled.

"Neither of you has ever flown. You have never seen the world through a bird's eye. Soaring, suspended by invisible forces, I had nearly forgotten the sensation myself. For some time I remained lost in a headiness I cannot explain—untethered, unbound, but in the end, undone."

Unable to hold his tongue, Skilley broke in again. "Undone?"

"As I banked toward the Tower, a heavy gust of wind tossed me into a tailspin. In no short time I came to ground, landing hard upon the cobblestones of a dimly lighted alleyway. When I regained my wits, I saw the many luminous pairs of eyes, blinking, watching me from the dark corners."

Maldwyn studied Skilley warily for a moment, then returned to his story.

"Cats—most cats, I will say—have no common decency. The cowards lurked in the shadows until they were certain of my injuries.

"As they circled, two of the bolder ones came near enough to sniff about. Then one ginger-striped brute crouched and lunged. Already mangled from the fall, I had a time of it defending myself. Ordinarily a cat is no match for a raven. A raven will emerge the victor every time. But six cats? Seven? And me with a broken wing?"

"A ginger-colored cat, you say?" repeated Skilley, bristling with apprehension. He knew of only one such cat on Fleet Street.

"A ginger of enormous proportions. I remember him well—and I made certain he would never forget me."

Maldwyn clacked his beak a time or two, then his voice grew gentle.

"The human girl you call Nell determined the outcome that day. She emerged from the inn like an avenging angel—like Britannia herself—armed with a lid and a ladle. These she beat together to create such a noise that my attackers scattered into the gloom. Had she not appeared, I would not be here to tell you this tale."

Abruptly the raven turned to Pip. "So tell me," he demanded. "Since you now claim to believe my story, what plan have you devised to restore me to the Tower?"

CHAPTER TWENTY-TWO

Skilley tried to make a good show of mousing as he prowled the inn the next day. The smell of mice was everywhere, but fortunately, not a whisker in sight.

As Skilley stalked, the raven's tale intruded on his thoughts. The more he considered the situation, the more churlish he became. This Maldwyn had not been part of the bargain. How the devil were a cat and a mouse to smuggle a raven out of the inn—let alone stroll him past St. Paul's Cathedral and through the fish market at Billingsgate—and into the Tower of London?

Impossible.

Ridiculous to even consider it.

Deep into these ruminations, Skilley settled himself on a comfortable windowsill with a view of the street.

Mr. Dickens was at his usual station at a nearby table. Was it his imagination, or was the man watching him? Skilley'd done his best to ignore the fellow all morning. Despite this determined apathy, it seemed to the cat that whenever he turned his head in that direction, the man would avert his eyes, quickly look down, and begin scratching at the page before him.

From his sill, Skilley could see that every passionate motion of Dickens's hand thrust spidery lines of black ink across the paper.

What was the man doing?

And then, without warning, Dickens rose from his seat and ambled casually across the floor to join Skilley at the window. "How are you getting on then, Cat? Have you had your fill of mice today?"

The questions seemed congenial. An affectionate hand scratched around his ears and chin in such an expert fashion that Skilley relaxed quite involuntarily.

"And how fares your good friend, the mouse with the exceptional teeth?" This last remark was so softly spoken, Skilley was not certain he had heard it correctly.

Oh, my, he thought, *this human's instincts are those of a cat.*

As Dickens returned to his table, he called for a pot of strong tea.

Skilley refused to look in his direction. Instead he allowed his mind to revisit the startling information Pip had provided at the conclusion of Maldwyn's story.

It seemed that Queen Victoria's wrath at the apparent kidnapping of her oldest raven was now news throughout London. Secrecy had given way to urgency. According to Pip, the human public had been informed of the threat and Her Majesty's men were scouring London for the kidnapped raven. The five remaining ravens were under heavy guard.

Her Majesty suspected the French.

France had recalled their ambassador; diplomatic waters between the two countries were asimmer with renewed (and historic) accusations and distrust. There had even been whispers of war.

How, Skilley wondered, had Pip learned all this?

Egad.

Skilley snapped to attention when he spotted the little mouse Too scampering along a baseboard. With one leap he had her safely in his jaws.

"Good kitty," Henry said. "Keep those vermin at bay." He bent over and ruffled the fur on Skilley's back, as Mr. Dickens had done earlier. The cat was unaccustomed to such casual affections; he quite liked them.

The landlord straightened. "Where's Adele gone, then?" he asked, looking around peevishly.

Quickly, Skilley dropped Too alongside a knothole in the baseboard. She stamped her tiny foot and said in an indignant voice, "I wish you'd give some notice before you eat Too!"

In response, Skilley shoved her through the knothole and began grooming himself. No one seemed to have taken note of the exchange. He continued to lick his teeth and jaws as if after a pleasant little appetizer.

A barmaid shrugged in answer to Henry's inquiry about Adele and said, "She's off on some errand, I 'spect.

Perhaps she's having another go at the coal man."

Henry chuckled at that. "At least she keeps my purse in her interest."

It was then the front door flew open and the afore-mentioned Adele burst in, followed by a gust of frigid January wind.

Deftly, she kicked the door closed behind her. Then she opened her shawl. Nestled uneasily in the crook of her arm was a most disagreeable-looking cat.

"Only guess what I found slinkin' 'bout the alleyway? Bit o' luck, innit?" Adele chirped. Cradling the cat in her arms, she cooed, "This 'ere's Oliver. I christened 'im in honor of our Mr. Dickens." She held the cat up for all to admire.

Skilley could only stare in alarm.

The alarm turned to dread as his eyes met those of that pitiless malcontent, Pinch.

Pinch—Oliver?

Well, this was an unwelcome twist.

Skilley's mind rang with a series of rapid-fire thoughts:

How will I keep up with the mouse-catching farce,
...protect the mice from this bloodthirsty cat,
...and keep Pinch in the dark as to the presence of the raven?

Skilley knew Pinch hated unfinished business. Any hint of this raven in the inn would arouse the murderous cat's worst instincts.

Pinch shot Skilley a glance of pure contempt. He then sprang from Adele's grasp and alit on the floor with an easy grace, muscles rippling beneath the coat of ginger stripes.

I must warn Pip, Skilley thought.

He turned his back on Pinch as if this were an every-day encounter and stalked toward the stairs. His languid tail with its hooked end revealed no hint of his true distress. Only the twitch of his right front paw as he raised it to the first step could have betrayed him, if Pinch were the kind of cat who noticed such things.

But Pinch was not troubled by such subtleties. He lived for three things: to chase, to catch…and to devour. At Ye Olde Cheshire Cheese he had found a perfect hunting ground—unless Skilley acted swiftly.

CHAPTER TWENTY-THREE

"You don't understand," Skilley said. "You must warn your friends without delay. This cat is a killer."

"I believe you," Pip answered.

"Then call them all together!" hissed Skilley.

"To employ the signal again so soon might draw attention from the humans." Pip was pacing the boards, paws clasped behind his back. Ten steps and a turn, ten steps and a turn...

"There's no time to waste," pressed Skilley.

"Yes, yes. I understand. But we've outwitted cats before, you know. We have a greater challenge before us."

"Greater—?"

"Maldwyn. We must find a way to get him back. It is a conundrum, I grant you."

"A what?"

"Mmm? Oh, yes. A thousand pardons. A conundrum is an unsolvable puzzle. But, no fear, I'll solve this one. And then we'll return Maldwyn to his rightful place in the Tower or—"

"Forget the blasted Tower for a moment! Maldwyn is safe in the garret, out of view and out of reach. You mice, however, face a danger beyond your wildest terrors."

"I assure you that we can handle this...this cat." Pip stopped his pacing and waved a paw, as if to clear the air of flatulence.

"No." Skilley's voice was grim. "Not this cat."

Pip stiffened. His nose twitched. And then he dashed to the nearest crack in the wall and disappeared.

Skilley spun about. "Hello, Pinch," he said lightly.

"Who were you talkin' to up here?" Pinch craned his neck to peer around Skilley.

"Talking? Don't be ridiculous. I was ciphering."

"Ciphering?"

"Trying to figure out how many mice there are to share between the two of us."

"Ha! You thought I came here with a mind to *share?*"

"Of course not," countered Skilley with silky irony. "You came to single-handedly trap over ten thousand mice, no? I think, my friend, that you're taking your own reputation too seriously."

"You doubt my lust for mice?" Pinch rasped.

"No more than my own," said Skilley, glancing away.

Pinch snorted. "Hah! Well, skill is another thing altogether! Who was it dispatched every last mouse at the Drury Lane Theatre?"

"They were pups, Pinch. Hardly difficult hunting."

"And tender eatin' they were." He licked his jowls.

Skilley searched about for some way to redirect the conversation. "And...and what do you think of our landlord?"

"That bacon-faced aledraper? A dumb oaf if ever there were one."

"Well, that oaf will give us both the boot if we don't work together. Between us—"

"Between us?" The venom in Pinch's voice poisoned the very air.

"Pinch, even you can't hunt down ten thousand mice alone."

The other cat finally sat. He nodded, though his bottle-green eye still flashed a threat. "Do as you will, then. You've weaseled your way into my territory, now mind that you keep your stink away from me."

"Easy enough. This place is nothing but mice and warm hearths. But let me warn you, the rodents here are sly. You may go days without a glimpse of so much as a whisker. And your nose'll be of no use. Their scent is everywhere." As a devilish afterthought Skilley added, "I've had my best luck in the kitchen."

Pinch nodded. "I'll start there, then." With that, the prickly tomcat bounded away.

Skilley stared after him as he vanished down the stairwell.

"I see what you mean," came a whisper from the chink in the wall.

CHAPTER TWENTY-FOUR

"Where are we going?"

"A place where that pernicious friend of yours won't think to look for us," Pip called back.

"Pinch is no friend! I know of his taste for violence. Why, I've seen him rip the bowels—" Skilley regretted the thoughtless words at once. "I don't want you thinking I'm the same as Pinch. I—I crossed him when I could."

Pip nodded. "I believe you did. He's an old nemesis, then?"

"Nem—really, Pip, you must stop using these words!"

"Enemy." The mouse grinned.

"Then, why not just say enemy? We must get off this landing, or we'll be sure to be found by my neme...neme— by Pinch."

"Very well, and when we are safe, I'll tell you a story or two—in plain words."

Pip dropped to his four paws and scuttled up to the next landing, where the attic lay. As soon as Skilley caught up to him, the mouse was off again, up to the garret landing and past Maldwyn's closed door. Before them was an iron ladder, bolted to the wall. It led to a casement window.

Pip was up and out in a blink.

Scaling a ladder was a harder task for a cat. Suffice it to say, he reached the top feeling spent and edgy. Digging his claws firmly into the soft, rotting wood of the window frame, he heaved himself after the mouse...

...and onto the rooftop of Ye Olde Cheshire Cheese.

It was nightfall.

And it was glorious.

"Welcome to my sanctuary. That is...my safe place."

Skilley stared out at the city and was dazzled. The sparkling lights of London were as bewitching a sight as ever he had witnessed. This, he thought—quite unexpectedly—was much like what Maldwyn had described: a view of the world through the eye of a bird. When his own eyes beheld the glistening silver ribbon the full moon had painted on the slow-flowing Thames, the enchantment was complete.

"How'd you find this place?" he whispered to Pip, never taking his eyes from the view.

"Nell, of course. She brought me here when we needed to be alone. I do miss her so."

"Nell?" He'd heard Maldwyn mention the name.

"The innkeeper's daughter. She saved my life the day my family was cruelly massacred by a cleaver—" Pip licked his paw—caught himself—then firmly tucked the paw under his arm. "In any event, it was Nell who taught me to read."

"To what?" Skilley asked, although he catalogued the bit about the cleaver in the back of his head. Cleavers, in his experience, rarely acted alone.

"To read. Nell taught me to read." Pip released a whimper of pleasure each time he uttered the word.

Skilley gave Pip a blank look.

"Oh, yes, of course. You don't know about reading. Why would you? And how can I explain what I don't entirely understand myself?" Pip stroked one ear.

"Let me think. Ah, yes! Remember the newspaper? The one I was standing on just before I dashed off to call on Maldwyn? You see, those lines and marks and dots on the paper are the humans' silent way of communicating. It's all around if you look. On papers and doors and windows…"

In a flurry of memory, the signs and crumpled handbills that Skilley had ignored every day of his life began to take on meaning. "But how did you—"

"I told you. Nell," Pip repeated. "It happened quite serendipitously—pardon, what I mean to say is, by accident. She was reading a book in her bed one evening. It was a volume by Mr. Dickens, who's often a guest in our very own chop room. Nell liked to read aloud and that's how I learned a good many fine human words. Why I remember one time when she patiently explained the meaning of the word irony—"

"Ahem!"

"Of course. I'm getting ahead of the story. Nell would hate that." Pip settled back on his haunches and tapped his chin with the tip of his tail.

"Let's see, then. Well, the night began like any other. I was nestled quite happily on her shoulder, following her finger as it tracked the words on the page, a peculiar habit of hers. I'd noticed for some time that the marks on the paper were distinctive:

One looked like a cross on a church steeple…

another like a fish hook I once saw Croomes pull from the mouth of a scrod…

and another like the round belly on our Henry."

Pip smiled at that image. "It became a game to learn them, one by one. And then it simply happened. I understood that each mark had its own sound. Strung together they made longer sounds.

"But that evening changed everything. I was following Nell's hand on the page, when in a moment of blinding clarity I knew the word hovering above her finger."

"What was it?" interrupted Skilley, now drawn into the tale.

"Handkerchief."

"What?"

"Handkerchief. It's a thing humans use—"

"I know what a handkerchief is. I've seen Adele's. Get on with the story."

"Very well." Pip gave a little huff. "I was so astonished that I raced down her arm, which made her squeal and drop the book. Fairly flying across the counterpane, I slid down the bedpost, scurried up to her dressing table, and began to run mad circles around her very own handker—"

"Brilliant! Did she understand?"

"Not at first. But she leapt from her bed and leaned over the dressing table. I held up a corner of the linen square and she let out a cry: 'Handkerchief! Is that what you're trying to tell me, Pip? You...you understand words?'

"I bobbed my head up and down. She shook her head, not quite believing. Then she said, 'hair ribbon.' Well, I dove into her little porcelain box and emerged with a mustard-colored hair ribbon between my teeth. She blinked at me in amazement. After a pause, she leaned down and whispered, 'Nell,' and I rested my paw on her cheek.

"That tender moment lasted no longer than a mouse's heartbeat. She jerked away and looked at me, shaking her head. 'But I never said the word handkerchief aloud,' she exclaimed. 'I never read that far—'

"She slowly backed away. Never taking her eyes from me, she lowered herself to the floor. Her fingers cast about for the book. Walking toward me with its pages trembling in her outstretched hands, she spoke very softly. 'Now, here's the page,' she said. 'See if you can find the word on your own, that's a good boy.'

"I crawled onto the open book, found the word, and gave it a friendly pat."

"What did she do?" asked Skilley.

"Why, she swooned. Dead away. It was awful."

Skilley's head bolted up. "*Dead* away?"

Pip nodded and wiped his eyes. "She's gone now. But I still see her sometimes," he said, sounding a little more cheerful.

"See her often, do you?" Skilley wasn't sure how he felt about sharing his home with a ghost, no matter how kindhearted she might be.

"Not often enough for my liking. I must tell her what I've discovered about Maldwyn."

"You still *talk* to her?"

"I try, but, well, you know humans. They just don't have the ears for it. She used to set out a newspaper, and I would paw at words. Of course, she can't do that, now that she's...gone. In any event, that's what inspired her to teach me to write."

"To what?"

"To make the marks myself," Pip added with reverence. "It's called *writing*."

A thought neatly unfolded itself in Skilley's mind,

laying itself out as plainly as a sheet of paper. "Is...is that what Mr. Dickens has been doing in that notebook of his?"

"Why, yes, it is. How I would love to have a glimpse at his words!"

"Well, why don't you?"

Pip looked at Skilley in horror. "Oh, I couldn't. To spy on an artist's unfinished work? That might well be a sin beyond forgiveness."

CHAPTER TWENTY-FIVE

It became obvious to Skilley that Pinch was set to conquer the inn in much the same fashion in which he had seized control of Fleet Street alleyways: brutish power. If anyone showed kindness toward the tomcat, he responded with characteristic violence. Soon, all save Adele were giving him a wide berth.

As Skilley well knew, this disregard for all tender feelings had been beat into Pinch by his former master. The man was a foul-tempered cur who had been hanged for the murder of a poor scrivener—and all for what? A handful of shillings and a silver watch with no fob chain. Pinch had watched his master's execution without flinching; uncountable beatings delivered by the man twitching at the end of the rope had hammered all trace of pity out of him. Pinch once confessed to Skilley that he had found the hanging quite satisfying.

With good reason, Henry seemed a trifle afraid of the cat. Only once did he try to pet the animal, but the snarl that greeted his outstretched hand quickly made him change his mind, and he withdrew with his fingers still intact. "Ah, well then," he muttered. "I suppose if Adele insists, we must keep you."

And Croomes, despite Skilley's best hope, did not banish Pinch from the inn. Rather, she kept a watchful eye on him whenever he entered the kitchen. The closest thing to a commentary on the new mouser Skilley had heard from her were these muttered words: "From tolerable to fragile, that's where things have gone. From tolerable to fragile." Skilley knew it could not be Pinch she considered fragile. So what had the woman so worried?

Only Adele doted on the new addition to the staff. And for some reason, Pinch accepted her scratching of the fur behind his ears. It was as if a bond of understanding had grown between them overnight—perhaps it was their common hatred of mice.

"Blest if I ain't pleased to have ya 'ere, Mr. Oliver," she said. "Them mouses was givin' me the apoplexies. Not that the other kitty weren't doin' of 'is best. There's just too many of 'em, see?"

Fortunately for Skilley's little friends, Pinch had no success at all catching mice.

It so happened that Mr. Dickens himself played a role in depriving Pinch of his best chance at a kill.

Wilkie Collins had been feeling under the weather, and so Dickens had spent several evenings at the inn without his friend. One particular night, the frustrated writer had devoted himself to nursing a dark mood. Adele,

Henry, and even Croomes, by unspoken agreement, had stayed well clear of him. The only lightening of Dickens's disposition occurred when he spied the small toothy mouse pulling an even smaller mouse by the tail toward a chink in the baseboard. Once the young one was secured behind the opening, the first mouse re-emerged and scanned the room.

"Collected all the wayward children, have you?" Dickens called softly. "You are wise to take such care. This new cat is nothing like your friend, the blue."

The mouse cocked his head to the side and considered the man before taking a few halting steps forward. This move was very nearly his undoing.

Pinch was a blur of ginger, and he had the mouse in his claws in a beat of Dickens's heart. But the writer, in his turn, was on Pinch a split second later, twisting the cat's ear with such force that the creature yowled and clawed at the man's hand. This allowed the mouse to scurry for the safety of the writer's shoe.

Pinch escaped the man's grasp and released a hideous and prolonged hiss.

"Off with you now!" snapped Dickens. "Find yourself another mouse. I've grown rather fond of this one." He took a threatening step toward the cat, who fled the room. Then in one movement the man scooped up the mouse.

"Cross me when I'm in the thick of a new novel, will he?" he growled. The hand that delivered Pip to his mouse hole was strong and warm. "Stay out of his way, will you? I know a little of stories, my fine friend, and this one could come to a tragic end."

Skilley was not pleased when he heard the tale from Pip. He knew that a thwarted Pinch was a dangerous Pinch. These days this disposition was only distinguishable from his normal mood by the choleric spasm about his left eye.

When Skilley saw Pinch at the end of the third day, he couldn't resist asking: "Any luck?"

"You mind your own traps." Then the ginger cat stalked away to continue his fruitless hunt.

Skilley was exhausted. Despite a warm hearth and the generous quantities of cheese the grateful mice were providing, this playacting was draining his strength. It could not be maintained. He had just closed his eyes for a quick doze when he heard squeals. Several young mice were gleefully sliding down a drainpipe. In plain view! Skilley had to talk to Pip. He set out to search for the mouse in all the usual places. Near the upstairs landing he heard unmistakable scuttling sounds.

Again, mice out in daylight.

Hadn't Pip warned them?

Skilley bounded up the last few steps.

Newspapers from days before remained scattered on the floor. Light from the afternoon sun filtered through the slats of the boarded windows, setting the paper ablaze with flashes of orange and gold.

"Pip," Skilley called as loudly as he dared. "Is that you?"

He was surprised by a startled cough from the corner. Another mouse. Ah. He remembered him as the wrinkled fellow with the matchstick cane. Old Bodkin, wasn't it?

"Have you seen Pip?" Skilley asked.

The old mouse seemed embarrassed, as if he'd been caught doing something he oughtn't.

"Well, umm… Who? Pip? No, haven't the foggiest. Pip who?"

He backed off the newspaper and swung his cane in a nervous arc. "Pip's not here. Why would he be here?

There's nothing here for him. Or me. Or any of us. Maybe we should leave."

Skilley's eyes narrowed with suspicion. "What have you been up to?"

"Up to? Nothing. Besides, I can't read anyway. Not like Pip. Not a whit like Pip. In fact, not at all. Though I try. It's simply beyond…"The fellow threw up his paws in resignation. "If you must know, I was just trying to decipher the news, but I'm nothing more than an old fool to think—"

Skilley rolled his eyes heavenward.

This mysterious reading business again.

He would never understand mice.

"By the by," asked Bodkin, "what were you wanting with Pip?"

"Only to make sure he's warned all your kith and kin. They must stay hidden. May I remind you that he eats mice."

"Yes, yes. We've been warned."

"I didn't see the gaslight flicker."

"Ah. We've other ways of passing news. Ways even older than the gaslight." Bodkin was paying Skilley only cursory attention now; he was engrossed in the act of turning up a corner of the paper with his matchstick, studying first one side, then the other.

"Such as?" Curiosity raised its feline head again.

"Word of Mouse, of course," said Bodkin, dropping the paper and looking quite grave now. "Although, I'll say

I am a bit worried. Some of the youngsters still don't grasp their peril."

"And you do, do you?" asked Skilley. "That'd explain why you're out in the open. What if I'd been Pin—"

"Oh, pish-posh. I'm an old mouse. What would your friend want with me?"

"*Your bones, to pick his teeth with.* And he won't care that they are old and brittle. Is that clear enough for you?"

A chastened Bodkin fiddled with his beard. "Er, yes, quite clear. How may I be of help?"

"Just do me the favor of warning your youngsters, by whatever means you wish."

"Very well. I am yours to command."

With that, Bodkin hobbled toward a hole in the wall, muttering to himself. "Ten thousand mice, afraid of one cat? Solidarity is what we need. Why I'd lead the charge myself…"

His last words were lost amongst the plaster panels and wooden laths.

CHAPTER TWENTY-SIX

"Not fair! I called Queen's Cross!"

"Stop this instant!" Pip ordered the youngsters who were scurrying up and down the cellar shelves, playing at whisker tag. "You must keep hidden. There is danger about."

The little ones only laughed.

"He's just another cat," sang one.

"Like Skilley!" chimed in another.

"No! Not in the least like Skilley! How can I make you see?" Pip's own brush with Pinch had been enough to awaken his every cell to the peril these pups were in. How could he make them feel it, too?

He grabbed the closest tail and yanked. Too flew backward and landed on her rear.

"Pip pulled Too's tail again. Bad mouse!" she bawled.

"Hush!" Pip cried. "And the rest of you: Behind the walls! Now!" Though he had no children of his own, he used the voice of an angry parent.

A frantic scuttering ensued, and soon Pip was left alone with one wailing youngster. Nervously sniffing the air for Pinch's unmistakable acrid scent, he took Too by the paw and led her to the nearest hole.

"There, there," he said, softening. "I do apologize, my dearest Too, but you must understand, this is not a game—"

"Pip, come quick!" cried Nudge, one of the scouting mice Pip had set to watch for the cat. He was a lanky, good-natured mouse, whose face had never before registered such absolute fear.

"What is it?" Pip's heart jounced, then bounced, then nearly stopped at the panic in Nudge's face.

"It's got Smeech and Popkin and I think Brummel. They wouldn't listen to me. They said they couldn't stand hiding anymore; they were dying for a bit of something sweet. And now—"

"Take me to them," Pip commanded. His words worked as a dash of icy water, bringing Nudge back to himself.

"Yes, sir. In the stillroom."

Long before they arrived, the terror from the still-room swept out to meet them. Hysterical mice poured forth, blocking their path. Pip and Nudge had to fight their way forward, as if swimming upstream through a water pipe.

"Excuse me, pardon me, please, let us pass." Pip's polite words were lost on the frenzied crowd. Finally, he turned his shoulder and plowed his way through to the chink in the wall—the passageway that in all times past had led to shelf after shelf of jams and jellies and sugary treats. This time, however, no sweetness awaited them.

Pip's trepidation was well justified.

"In there, sir," Nudge whispered. "Something awful."

Pip quashed the nausea that threatened to overcome him and crept through the narrow opening.

What he saw made him quake from his nose to the very tip of his tail. Smeech and Popkin were already gone. And Brummel…nearly so.

It was the sight of Bodkin racing across the floor, brandishing his cane like a sword, that stopped his heart cold. Who would have thought one so old could move with such swiftness? Before Pip could call to him, the brave fool had attacked the cat, stabbing at his paw again and again with his matchstick.

Pinch now turned all his bloodthirsty attention toward this feeble threat.

Pip scrambled toward the old mouse. "Bodkin!" he cried. He stumbled, then fell, paralyzed by the sight that so violently seized him. "Bodkin," he whimpered.

He could do nothing.

He was, after all, only one mouse.

Murder and mayhem at The Cheese!

I'd returned the other afternoon from one of my invigorating walks to discover that Adele had brought in another mouser. I still bear the scars of my own encounter with the bully. Unlike the blue I've grown so fond of, this one appears a perfect ruffian. Adele has spent the last quarter-hour mopping up the gruesome remnants of his first kill. Rather untidy for a cat.

He brings to mind my own Bill Sykes. I still shrink at the memory of committing his heartless perfidy to pen and ink. How could I have allowed him to so brutally slay poor Nancy?

Ah, well, a writer must never shy away from a good, solid, literary murder. He must be merciless. If the story necessitates, he must hang the antagonist, drown the heroine, commit the parson's long-suffering wife to Bedlam—and damn the reviewers!

But I fritter my time when I should be writing the first installment of my next serialization. My Sydney Carton must face the guillotine. This tale of two cities could be my best yet, but I am still in need of a smart phrase to begin it.

I hope for the best, but expect the worst.

CHAPTER TWENTY-SEVEN

It took time to coax the story out of Nudge, but Skilley was patient.

The ghoulish tale emerged from the distraught mouse between nervous sips of spider leg tea (a popular mouse remedy for shock). Poor Nudge told the story in gasps, accompanied by the occasional curse, which was brought down quite colorfully on Pinch's head. Each new invective was followed by yet another gulp of tea and a bite of cheese (a mouse remedy for nearly everything). When Nudge was done, Skilley felt the hackles rise along his back.

He had one question.

"And what of Pip? Is he, was he...?"

Nudge swallowed, then shook his head vigorously. Pip was not hurt. He'd last seen him heading up...

But Skilley was already on his way.

CHAPTER TWENTY-EIGHT

Within moments Skilley found himself on the rooftop of Ye Olde Cheshire Cheese.

Ah, London.

The sooty air, a source of complaint to most of the city, was an elixir to the street cat. He took several pleasurable breaths before his eyes fell on the glimmering Thames. Tonight the moon's reflection across the water reminded him of spilt milk.

Remembering Pip, he tore his gaze away and scanned the rooftop. He spied his friend huddled, shivering, against the old brick chimney. Skilley was not surprised that the mouse was shaking so violently. The wind was cold, it is true, but the loss of several young mice—and then Bodkin—would have made him colder still.

"Pip!"

The mouse looked up with a blank expression. Upon seeing Skilley, the look instantly changed to one of relief. Skilley, who lacked Pip's ease with words, was unsure how to respond. He trotted over and—with the greatest care—scooped the mouse up into his mouth. This made speaking marvelously difficult.

As for Pip, traveling in the cat's mouth no longer felt strange to him, and he went along without protest.

Skilley carried him to the sheltered side of the chimney, away from the blustery wind. Ever so gently, he set Pip down.

"We'll take cover here for a bit. I'll warm you up in my paws, if you like," suggested Skilley. He wouldn't have blamed Pip for declining the offer. *In his place*, Skilley thought, *I might not feel kindly toward cats of any stripe today.*

Pip surprised him.

"I accept your offer, and thank you. I admit to feeling rather chilled. It's propitious that you should happen along just now." Pip shuddered again.

"Propi—? Never mind."

"Lucky," said Pip with a weak smile.

Skilley circled the spot once and dropped to the cold slate alongside the chimney. He then tucked in his hind legs and opened his front paws, looking for all the world to Pip like the great Sphinx of Egypt, a mysterious statue he had seen in one of Nell's books.

"You really are an enigma—a perfect puzzle of a cat."

"Are you coming or not? I can hear your teeth rattling from here. And keep to words a street cat understands, would you?" said Skilley, not without humor.

Pip skittled between the cat's outstretched front legs. Skilley drew in his paws, enveloping the mouse in a cozy circle of fur.

After adjustments were made for the sake of comfort, each grew still and sighed in his turn. It had been an unforgivably long day.

"I'm—I'm sorry about your friends," murmured Skilley. Then he added, "Do you understand now why Pinch is a much greater problem than restoring Maldwyn to his place?"

"Mmm. He's certainly a more rapacious one, I'll grant you that." The second reference to the day's tragedy brought on an inevitable fit of grooming.

Pip licked his paw…

flicked his ear…

licked his paw…

and brushed his whiskers.

Skilley watched, making no comment.

When Pip paused for a moment, Skilley said softly, "I'm sorry I wasn't there."

Pip gave his paw another quick lick—and stopped short of rubbing his nose. "No, but I was. In any case, even if I had reached Bodkin's side in time, what could I have done? That's the trouble with being a mouse. One hasn't the size, you see, of one's enemies. If a friend is in mortal danger—" He stopped. Taking a deep breath, Pip returned to his ritual.

He licked his paw…

touched his belly—

"Stop!" cried Skilley, startling Pip. "Please. I know you feel dreadful. But you're right. There was nothing you could do. You are small...but you are not alone." Skilley wrestled with the pang of guilt he felt for not shadowing Pinch more closely.

"Neither are you," offered Pip.

"Why, er, thank you, Pip," said Skilley. "Of course." And with that, Pip curled up under Skilley's chin.

The day, which had left them spent and fatigued, took its final toll; the cat drew his paws in a bit tighter, gently cradling the mouse, and soon, both were snugly and soundly asleep under a waxing English moon.

And that's just how Pinch found them.

CHAPTER TWENTY-NINE

"Well, well, well, what's this?" oozed Pinch in a voice as sticky sweet as honey. He crouched inches from Skilley's nose, eyes locked on Pip, who was fast asleep between his friend's paws, blissfully ignorant of the threat.

"This one's mine," hissed Skilley, grateful for the bolt of inspiration. Moments before, he had wakened from a deep slumber to a sensation of cold terror. Pinch's sour scent had given him just enough time to react.

Pinch edged closer, but at the sight of Pip's inert form, he recoiled. "Ugh. It's dead! What kind of cat are you?"

"I-I like them that way." Skilley's every nerve was on alert.

Perhaps you can sleep when two cats are arguing just above your head, but Pip could not. And because he could not, he awoke, to find himself looking directly into a pair of venomous green eyes.

"I thought you said 'e was dead." Pinch was electric with suspicion.

Without pausing to deliberate, Skilley gave way to instinct. With one brutal swipe of a paw, he smacked Pip with such force that the little mouse flew across the rooftop.

"Now he is!" Skilley snarled.

For one suspended instant, no one moved.

Pinch stared at Skilley, his look unreadable.

Skilley looked to Pip, who stared back with a mixture of terror and confusion.

To his relief, Pip scrambled onto all fours and tore toward the open window.

"What was *that* about, I'd like t'know?" demanded Pinch. But he was talking to himself.

Skilley was gone.

CHAPTER THIRTY

Pip had the advantage in that he knew every crack, crevice, and hidey-hole in the old inn. The mouse could not—and would not—be found until he was ready, that much was clear. Skilley had questioned various other mice, but to no avail. It was Too who brought home the futility of finding his erstwhile friend.

Skilley came across the tiny mouse on the garret landing, where she was happily playing with a plump lemon seed.

"You shouldn't be out in the open like this," Skilley said irritably.

"Is Skilley going to pull Too's tail?" she asked in a voice of accusation. Then her expression changed to one of exaggerated severity. "What did Skilley do to make Pip sad? No, no. Too won't tell you where he is. Pip is busy." She went back to her lemon seed, cooing to it, "There, there, don't cry now."

"But I need to find him. Something's happened and I don't know what to do."

"Why don't you ask *that one?*" she said, pointing over her shoulder at Maldwyn's door. "*He* knows everything."

Skilley stared at the door that hung loosely on its hinges. A slight push of his nose was all that stood between him and the dreadful old bird. Did he dare?

He snapped his tail and thrust out his chest. "Very well. I will ask Maldwyn."

But as soon as he eased through the entrance to the garret room, his nerve began to fail him.

"You?" The ancient bird looked down his iron-black beak and regarded Skilley with an inscrutable look; there was no guessing what lay behind it.

"Please, sir…" Skilley hesitated, then plowed ahead. "I need your advice."

"My advice, you say? How very thoughtful of a cat to consider a raven's advice."

Skilley nearly turned away at that. "Well, I have a—"

"Yes, yes, you have troubles. Of course, you do. And you've come to me because you've heard I am known to be—how would one phrase it?"

"Wise?" offered Skilley, chancing that a bit of flattery might soften the old bird.

"Inclined to see through falsehood would be more accurate. The lies one tells oneself are the worst, of course. No, no, no." He waved a wing dismissively. "Don't tell me a thing. I can guess readily enough. You've already turned on young Pip, have you?"

Skilley was stunned. "*He told you?*"

"Don't be absurd. He's too fond of you for that; although with these recent developments, who's to know? Then again, Pip is one of these new radical thinkers who believe that any creature"—here the raven paused and turned a bead of an eye toward Skilley—"even a cat, can be rehabilitated. But, to answer your question, no, he did not speak of any troubles to me."

"Then how did you—?"

"You are a cat."

Skilley offered no apologies. Could one apologize for one's being? This visit had been a bad idea. For all his grizzled wisdom, Maldwyn's hatred of felines made him a poor choice for a confessor.

"Yes, I am a cat, and clearly unwelcome here." Skilley turned to leave.

"And Pip is a mouse," the raven called after him. "What other outcome did you expect? Cats and mice are enemies eternal."

Skilley spun around and stared angrily at the raven. "Cats and mice, you say? But what of *one* cat and *one* mouse? I say they can be friends if they choose."

"You're the one who turned against your so-called friend," snapped the raven, "not I."

"I was trying to protect him." The moment the words left his mouth, Skilley knew they were a lie. And the way Maldwyn cocked his head proved that he knew it, too.

"What I mean is," Skilley continued, "I wasn't going to eat him. I was just pretending..." He groped vainly for the right words. He tried to remember everything that had occurred the other night, in particular, the thoughts that had passed through his head when Pinch surprised them on the roof.

He told the raven the story.

He held back nothing.

Then he waited. The raven's response was not long in coming.

"As I have already observed," said Maldwyn, "you're a cat. An *alley* cat, an infernal subspecies. I know your kind. Look at me." He held up his crippled wing, once broken, now poorly mended. He strutted and stumbled forward, closer to Skilley, then thrust his beak into his face. "And it took a cowardly gang of your friends to do this. Yes, I know your kind."

"Those were no friends of mine."

"Perhaps you weren't one of that savage rabble. And yet—" Maldwyn paused to stab at a beetle scurrying across the boards. He tossed his head back to swallow the insect, then said matter-of-factly, "And yet, when confronted with the possible discovery of your secret, you gave in to your nature, did you not?"

Skilley was in no mood to be lectured. "As you have just given in to yours, by eating that unfortunate insect?

What do you suppose it felt toward you in that instant?"

"Ah. But I made no pretense of friendship," scored the raven.

"I was not pretend—"

Skilley could not finish the sentence. He felt a cutting pain, yet he assured himself he owed neither Pip nor Maldwyn an explanation. Had he not kept his end of the bargain? Why, the ingrates should thank him for all that he had done to protect them thus far! They should shower him with cheese and compliments. As for Pip...

This was of course, the very sort of drivel that even a sensible person grasps at to console himself when he is utterly and undeniably in the wrong.

And though not a person, Skilley was sensible. As if through a looking glass, quite suddenly he saw the truth in himself.

"Yes," said the raven. "I see."

No sound from Skilley.

Only the clickering of Maldwyn's claws, as he awkwardly shifted his stance, cut through the heavy silence.

At last Maldwyn spoke again. His head tilted to one side, then the other. "Don't tell me you feel sorry for what you've done?"

More silence.

"Interesting. Suspect, but interesting."

More clickering followed as the bird hopped and

hobbled around Skilley. "Well, you certainly *look* the alley cat. Those are some nasty scrapes and scars—which perhaps explains why you behaved like an alley cat."

When at last Skilley spoke, he felt unspeakably tired. "I acted to save my own hide. I didn't want Pinch to know of my, my—"

"Your unseemly love of cheese?"

"No!" said Skilley. His agitation at being so misunderstood drove the words from his mouth in a rush. "I didn't want him to know that Pip was—"

"Yes? Go on. Say it."

"—my friend. I didn't mean to hurt him. Pip, I mean."

The raven blinked several times and then said, "Even more remarkable to me is the fact that I believe you. I also believe that you did hurt him. And now you feel sorry and wonder how you can undo what's been done, eh? Well, I am here to tell you that you cannot undo it any more than I can fly back to the Tower on my own and resume my rightful place. Only worms and insects have no memories of past sins. And only humans can choose to forget them. We animals must live with our foolhardy choices."

Had Skilley detected a change in Maldwyn's tone?

"All one can do"—the bird's tone *had* softened—"is own up to the truth."

"The truth," Skilley spat, "is that I should never have come to The Cheese."

Maldwyn's head snapped up at that. He clacked his beak. "And if you hadn't, and we now had only Pinch's fine company? I know of his brutality most intimately. He it was who took my eye. You are a cat, but that one...that one is a fiend."

"A cat is a cat," said Skilley.

Maldwyn remained quiet for a long while, deep in thought. When at last he spoke, the hardness in his good eye seemed to melt away and his voice rasped in his throat. "And nature can't be changed?" He turned his back, as if dismissing the humbled cat.

Skilley felt positively peevish now. "I don't know why I came to you."

With his back still turned, Maldwyn answered. "You knew before you entered this chamber that you would receive no soft words from me. Therefore, you must have come in search of the truth."

Then Maldwyn gathered himself and stood erect. Once more Skilley witnessed the rising majesty of a Tower raven. Even with his head averted, there was royalty in his form.

"You want the truth, Master Skilley? Then find out just what manner of cat you really are...and brazenly, unabashedly, boldly, be that cat."

The bird shrank to his normal self, which left him looking old and impossibly frail. "Kindly leave now. You have wearied me."

CHAPTER THIRTY-ONE

February, the shortest of all months of the year, surprised London with an unseasonable thaw. A springlike warmth caused the city's inhabitants to abandon their great coats and scarves and to sally forth in search of adventure.

No such thaw, however, descended upon Ye Olde Cheshire Cheese. Pinch turned surlier as the mice took greater care to avoid him. Absurdly, he accused Skilley of catching all of them on the sly.

"Don't cast the blame on me," Skilley said. "They're too frightened of you to show themselves. It may be time for you to turn to easier work—perhaps at the wharf? There's fish heads aplenty for a skilled hunter such as yourself."

"Leave the Cheese? Not of me own doing! Though I'm sick to death of table scraps. I'll not stomach another plate of bubble and squeak. Might nip me a bit of cod tonight when that cook closes shop for the night."

"I'd steer clear of her if I were you," warned Skilley. "She'll have your guts for garters if she catches you stealing from her kitchen."

Croomes, for her part, was a storm that each day broke earlier and blew harder. She ranted and raved about the dwindling stores of cheese. "It's more than the usual deficit!" she cried, but when pressed, the cook could offer Henry no further explanation.

How was she to know that on top of the inn's mice she was also nightly feeding a rather large cat?

Poor Henry suffered Croomes's tirades with painful resignation. And Adele? If Pinch had her skill for uncovering mice, he would have dined in great state. As it was, Adele was left to doubt her own sanity.

"Why does no one else see 'em?" she lamented.

As for Skilley, he had not run across Pip since the affair on the roof. Then one morning he caught sight of him scrambling up a drainpipe, sporting what looked like a boot-blackened tail. He called to him, but Pip had already scrambled away.

Fretful and unabsolved, Skilley took to visiting Maldwyn. Not that the visits were always pleasant. Indeed, they were almost always the opposite.

Despite this, Skilley found himself growing fond of the old curmudgeon. Maldwyn made him use his brain, and though this experience often proved exhausting— and sometimes painful—their conversations left Skilley feeling alert, even electrified, for hours afterward.

"Maybe I should talk to Pip," he said to Maldwyn one rainy afternoon.

"If you think it would help."

"What do you think?"

"I think I'd like another nip of sugar." The old raven had settled himself in a pile of rags and straw, his eyes closed, his beak opening and closing with each asthmatic breath.

"I'll fetch you one," said Skilley.

"If you think it would help."

"Isn't that what you want?"

"Does it matter what I want?"

Skilley rattled his head to shake out the confusion. "Well, then! What about Pip?"

"He can get his own sugar."

"That's not what I meant."

"But that's the correct answer." The bird buried his beak under his wing.

"You don't understand." But it was no use. Maldwyn's gesture was as good as a closed door. "All right then. I will talk to Pip."

Maldwyn seemed to make an even stronger point of ignoring the cat.

"I will. See if I don't," declared Skilley.

The raven sighed and had the last muffled word, coming, as it was, from under his wing. "What I'd like to see...what I'd love to see...what I'm dying to see, is *how you're going to return me to my rightful place in the Tower.*"

CHAPTER THIRTY-TWO

In the chop room Skilley ran into a thoroughly ruffled Pinch. His matted fur and bedraggled tail reeked of leeks and garlic, and a streamer of cress dangled between his eyes. Attached to his side was a sticky glob of wheat flour.

"Whatever happened to you?" Skilley asked, squelching an urge to burst into laughter.

Pinch simply hissed at him. Then out came the word "Croomes," uttered with such ill will it made Skilley wince.

The livid cat disappeared behind a drape, perhaps to clean himself.

"Best avoid the kitchen," Adele called to Skilley. "Cook's in a right state. She just flung a lump of pasty dough at my Oliver. And mind you, her aim is sure. But imagine! Accusin' the cat of stealin' 'er cheese!" She sniggered. "As if a cat'd touch cheese."

Skilley cringed, then hurried from the room and dashed down to the cellar. "Hsst. Pip," he whispered half-heartedly through one of the numerous mouse holes in the masonry walls. "Are you there?"

"He's in the attic." It was Too.

Her feathery whiskers emerged first, followed by her velvety ears. Pip was practicing his *ledders*, she explained.

"Ledders?" Skilley raised a brow.

"Ledders is what he calls 'em, and ledders is what they be," said Too. "His ledders."

Skilley made a move to the stairs.

"And he 'stinctly said he doesn't want to be 'sturbed."

"Oh, all right! I won't 'sturb—"

Too gave a brief cry and popped back into the hole without having to be told.

When Skilley turned around he saw why.

Pinch!

A full half-page of newspaper had fastened itself to the hardening lump of dough on his side. The paper showed the shredded evidence of his claws, but still it stuck stubbornly to the dried paste and matted fur as if it were now a permanent part of Pinch's hide.

Skilley had to stop himself again from laughing out loud as the indignant cat slunk away, no doubt to find some private spot to continue his fruitless grooming.

CHAPTER THIRTY-THREE

Making a mess of things is an occupation at which even the most unskilled can excel. But mending is an art that requires years of practice. In short, breaking a thing is easy (even a child can do it); fixing that selfsame thing may be harder (sometimes even adult persons cannot manage it).

Skilley was learning this lesson in the most painful of ways. What he had broken was a thread of trust as thin and delicate as a glass filament—a thread that had bound him to one of only two friends in his life.

Maldwyn's ear was better than none.

"I'm losing my mind," said Skilley in exasperation. "I call to him through the attic door but he says he is too busy. He speaks to everyone but me, and I spend all day talking to myself."

"Mmm. Seems everyone is talking to the wrong person." Maldwyn returned to filing his beak on the steel stays of an old abandoned corset.

"I will talk to him," said Skilley. "And tell him I'm sorry."

"So you keep threatening to do." The raven gave the metal stay another swipe with his beak, then paused. "But what are you sorry for?"

"For? Why, I'm sorry for what happened."

"What happened?" Maldwyn asked the question in a very uncurious way.

"What are you wittering on about? What happened on the roof, of course!"

"The roof?"

"What happened on the roof with Pinch. You heard my confession. You know what I'm talking about."

Maldwyn continued his Socratic approach, answering each question with another in return. "Ah. But, do you know what happened and why? And this is most important—do you know what in the name of all that is holy *you are supposed to be sorry for?*"

Maldwyn waited a full minute. "Well, have you no answer?"

"Haven't you?" Skilley challenged. "You, who are the nightingale with the golden beak? You have enough words to overflow the Thames. You and Pip—" At the mention of his lost friend, Skilley's voice cracked.

"Skilley." The raven rarely called him by name. "When one has done an injury to another, the simplest solution is to offer up that time-honored and most insulting olive branch, 'I'm sorry.' The speaker of these words is often bewildered when they are received with anything less than gushing gratitude. Can you imagine why?"

Skilley stared dully at Maldwyn. "I don't know what you're talking about."

"Very well, I will tell you. It is not enough to say you are sorry. You must utterly own the terrible thing you have done. You must cast no blame on the one you've injured. Rather, accept every molecule of the responsibility, even if reason and self-preservation scream against it. Then, and only then, will the words 'I am sorry' have meaning."

This time Skilley didn't wait for permission, but rather barged right in on the preoccupied mouse.

The spectacle that lay before him drove all other thoughts from his mind. He found himself fumbling to hold on to its slippery meaning. So this was what Too had meant when she said Pip was practicing his "ledders." The marks that covered the lowest four inches of the wall to his left looked something like this:

$$c \, d \, l \, f \, n \, x \, p \, g \, R \, y \, v \, w$$

Skilley followed the inky trail along two and a third walls. They led a scripted path to Pip, who was so engrossed in his task that he seemed unaware of his visitor. Either that, Skilley thought, *or he doesn't want to acknowledge my presence.*

"Pip, do you have a moment?"

"Dreadfully busy just now, Skilley."

"This is rather important."

"So is rescuing England and France from the brink of war." Pip dipped his tail in a thimble and brushed it onto the surface of the wall. He stepped back and appraised his work with dissatisfaction.

"Yes, yes, I see." Although Skilley didn't see at all. What could this silly obsession with writing possibly have to do with saving England? The cat wisely caught his own tongue and changed the subject.

"There is something I would like to say."

"I'm listening." Pip studiously applied his skills to a new mark; it appeared to Skilley very much like the ears on a cat. It looked something like this:

$$\mathcal{M}$$

Skilley braced himself before releasing the hailstorm of words that he had been holding in for so long.

"The other night, on the roof—"

Pip turned to begin another letter.

"Wait, Pip! Hear me out."

Skilley began again. "The other night on the roof... I betrayed you. I was terrified of what would happen if Pinch learned of our friendship. I was ashamed, I was selfish, and I was a coward. I hate that cat, yet I cannot divorce him from myself. And if I can feel such horror and disgust at what I did, how much more might you? You, who trusted me?"

Pip stopped writing and his eyes met Skilley's. The cat lowered his gaze, then continued.

"That night I learned an awful truth. There are things that once lost cannot be brought back. But whether you forgive me or not, I promise until the moment of my last mortal breath to be the cat you once believed me to be. I am sorry, Pip. Truly sorry."

Pip shot him a very small smile. "That's a good many words for a cat."

CHAPTER THIRTY-FOUR

As he watched Pip standing before the mouse council, Skilley's heart felt lighter than it had in days. He had humbly thanked Pip for including him in the gathering, but his friend had only shrugged and smiled.

The meeting place was a shadowy corner of the cellar, and Skilley was, as ever, on alert for signs of Pinch. Doxy, a rather self-important mouse, had arrived last, wiping his paws on his belly and reeking of cheese.

"Ahem." Toff, a senior member of the mouse council, cleared his throat in impatience. "Are we to proceed or not?"

Pip licked his paw...

touched his ear...

A quick glance from Skilley, followed by the slightest shake of his head, arrested Pip's nervous habit.

"Yes, yes, yes. We must proceed. I have called you all together"—here Pip nodded at the mice and then at Skilley—"to discuss Maldwyn."

Mumbles and grumbles of "not again," "not today," and "not on your cheese-eating life" swept through the dozen or so council members.

Pip disregarded the objections. Somehow he had to convince his fellow mice that a course of action must be agreed upon. *Posthaste.*

Skilley had no patience with the council members' grumblings. "Listen to Pip," he said. "He has a fine idea."

After the coughs, shrugs, and a surprising amount of snickering had died down, Pip continued. "I have been puzzling over the riddle of what to do with our friend Maldwyn for some time now.

"He cannot fly—that we know. He cannot walk to the Tower, unless we wish to draw out every brigand, cut-purse, and highwayman in all of London. Thanks to the human newspapers, the entire city is on the lookout for Maldwyn, and more than a few would leap at the opportunity to ransom the Queen's raven.

"Nor would we want to draw the attention of the constables. Our humans might be held responsible for the raven's presence, and I fear it would not go well with them if the Queen's men found him under this roof." Pip paused to catch his breath.

It was all the opening the council needed.

"What we have is a right pickle then," announced Doxy in his usual imperious tone.

"Picklelilly!" cried another. "What we have is pure picklelilly."

Shouts of "hear, hear" stuttered through the assembly.

"Be that as it may," Pip continued, shouting to be heard above the fray, "there is another solution we haven't discussed as yet. We only have need of paper and ink and a bit of luck."

"And a smattering of courage," added Skilley.

"And how about a bit of marmalade, while we're at it," called a rather cheeky mouse by the name of Chesterfield.

"And some filberts," ordered another.

"And toast!"

"Yes! Toast and marmalade!"

"And filberts!"

Pip could feel himself losing control of the council.

"Silence!" Skilley thundered. It was the same voice of command Pip had once used on him. "Hush, and listen to Pip. He knows what he's about. He has a plan. And it can work. He has more brains than the entire woolly-headed lot of you." Skilley rose and prowled around the council. "So give him, if you please, the courtesy of your ears. And I mean every ear."

The mice watched him nervously now. The recent experience with Pinch was obvious in their faces.

Not a twitter.

Not a hiccup.

Not a twitch of one solitary whisker.

Skilley laid himself down to the right of Pip and smiled sweetly at the now paralyzed congregation.

"*Woolly-headed?*" whispered Pip.

"Go on," said Skilley. "They're waiting,"

There were no further interruptions as Pip laid out the plan. He had just finished explaining the final steps when the tender skin beneath his fur prickled. Every mouse in the room was experiencing a similar sensation.

"Scatter!" Skilley cried, unnecessarily.

The mice whisked from the room in all directions, leaving behind tiny whirlwinds of empty dust.

Seconds later, Pinch appeared at the bottom of the cellar stairs. "So, this 'ere's the spot where you've been mousing alone, eh?" He sounded disinterested at first, as if he were asking after Skilley's digestion. "Well? Is it? Is this where they 'ide?" More insistent now, he stalked from hole to hole, sniffing and snorting. "Their reek is strong 'ere."

Skilley had prepared himself for this. "Yes! And you've just spooked the lot of them away!" he scolded. "There would've been plenty for us both, but you—"

"I wouldn't take that tone if I was you."

"Mercifully, I'm not you. My tone is my own, and I'll take it where I please—Piccadilly Circus, if I choose, although I suspect your tastes run more to the *slums of St. Giles.*"

Pinch, who had been keeping his legendary temper in check for days, let his claws spring from their pads. His tail snapped and burst into the shape of a chimney sweep's brush. His ears flattened against his head, and he hissed from the very back of his throat.

The low moaning snarl was the only warning Skilley had before Pinch catapulted himself at him. But it was enough. Skilley dodged to the right, which sent Pinch tumbling across the flagstones. He came to a rest against the far wall, his four feet splayed out about him.

"Why, you coward!" Pinch sprang up and charged.

Skilley evaded him again.

And again Pinch landed in a tumbled heap.

How is this possible? Skilley thought. *The other cat hasn't landed a single blow.*

The wonder of it almost made him forget that this was Pinch. *The most dangerous cat on Fleet Street.*

Although chilling, Skilley found the encounter, very ...familiar. *Aha!* he thought. *It's just like dodging a fishwife's broom!*

Skilley braced for another attack. But none came. He looked about and found himself alone.

Pinch had fled the room, yet oddly it was Skilley who felt the tingle of fear race down his spine.

CHAPTER THIRTY-FIVE

Pip had been incubating the idea for days now. He knew from observing the patrons of the inn that when humans were far from one another they often communicated through letter writing. The penny post, it was called. All they needed were paper, an envelope, and a stamp.

Pip's plan was bold but simple: a discreet letter would be sent to the Tower.

Nudge and Too were assigned to procure the paper and the envelope. Pip would provide his own practiced lettering. As neither Skilley nor Pip had thumbs with which to put the postal package together, they would leave that task to Maldwyn.

Being a raven, he was mightily gifted with his beak and claws.

As for acquiring the stamp, the mice and raven had naturally turned to Skilley. Among them, only he could move openly among the humans.

But if Skilley thought stealing a stamp would be simple, he was quickly disabused of that notion.

Wilkie Collins

One would think that a penny stamp would be easy to come by in this particular inn, what with so many writers bumping about: Mr. Dickens, Mr. Collins, a tall bull-dog of a man named Thackeray, and a Mr. Bulwer-Lytton, who seemed a bit full of himself. But one would be wrong. Writers are a miserly lot, and to leave something as dear as a penny red lying about was looked upon by these artists with nothing short of horror.

William Makepeace Thackeray

Edward Bulwer-Lytton

CHAPTER THIRTY-SIX

It was Mr. Thackeray's fondness for peppers, of all things, that gave Skilley the opportunity to carry out his task.

Cold had returned, reminding London's citizens of just how fickle the English climate could be.

On a particularly severe afternoon, Mr. Thackeray bustled into the inn, stamping his feet and shaking a dusting of snow from his cloak.

"Winter is the name of misery herself on the lips of all frost-battered creatures," he cried to Henry. "Pull me a pint. And a jigger of rum."

"Right up," Henry called. "You may take Mr. Dickens's table. He's not likely to brave the weather today."

Skilley dozed near the fireplace, grateful for his home in the inn. The warmth against his backside (and the fact that Pinch was off in some other room, likely hiding from Croomes) was a great comfort.

His ears pricked up when he heard Mr. Thackeray call out to the barmaid. "I've some letters to post," he said. "Adele, darling, could you run out and purchase a dozen penny reds?"

"What? Now? In this weather?"

"I'll give you tuppence for it."

"Tuppence? Make it 'alf a crown an' I'm your girl."

"Half a crown? Why for that I'd go myself! How about a shilling? And a kiss on the cheek?"

"Now 'ow is that payment fer me, eh? A shilling, no kiss, an' it's a bargain."

"Very well," Mr. Thackeray grumped. "No kiss then."

Adele bundled up and swept from the inn, laughing at the thought of a kiss from this older gentleman.

"Er, will you be ordering any supper, then?" asked Henry.

A whooping sort of cough and a belch rolled from Mr. Thackeray's throat. "Some toast perhaps. And cheese, of course. Your famous Cheshire. And do you have any peppers? I would love some peppers—red and spicy, if you have them."

"But my dear Mr. Thackeray," Henry said with some reluctance (Thackeray was, after all, a good patron), "you know how they upset your digestion."

"Blast my digestion," the writer cried. "I've never known anyone to die of dyspepsia. Since I'm not to have a kiss, I want some peppers."

"As you wish. Toast and cheese…and peppers. Red and spicy."

Then to a passing potboy Henry whispered, "Be ready for Vesuvius."

The potboy scratched his head and shrugged. He bent down to pet Skilley behind the ears. "What the blazes is Vess-poo-chee-us?"

Skilley had no answer to that question. But he knew a great deal about peppers. He'd tried to eat one once. The first bite of pepper had sent him into shudders of burning pain. And when he'd tried to rub the tears from his eyes with paws that had touched the savage vegetables, his agony made him wish for a relief that he assumed only death could provide. Skilley was wrong; time alone had proved an effective remedy.

Peppers. He believed he hated them second only to doors.

He stared at Mr. Thackeray, who now sat at Mr. Dickens's table, scribbling away on sheets of paper. *Writing*, Pip had called it. Though Pip did it with his tail, this man used a goose quill. While Skilley was wondering what had become of the goose that had once been attached to that quill, Henry produced a plate of cheese and roasted peppers.

Mmmm. Now Skilley remembered why he had tried the peppers. They smelled fine. A perfect companion aroma to the cheese. Sweet, yet pungent, tangy and fruity all at once. A perfect disguise to the firestorm they held inside.

Mr. Thackeray carefully built a cheesy structure upon a foundation of toast. The capstone was a full red pepper, curved into what appeared to be a smile.

A smile of deceit.

In two bites, the writer devoured the construct, smile and all.

His nose flushed crimson.

His bulldog cheeks quivered.

The veins on his forehead nearly popped and beads of sweat formed, then swelled, then trickled down his nose and cheeks.

"Delicious," he croaked. With years of experience as a practiced pepper eater, he wiped his eyes not with his hands but with a silk handkerchief.

He was just building his second course when Adele returned with the stamps.

"An even dozen," she said. "Already cut an'—What's this? Why, Mr. Thackeray, 'ave you been at them peppers again?"

"I'm sorry, my dear, but I just can't resist."

"You're as red as these 'ere penny stamps," she exclaimed. Then she laughed. "You're as red as me Uncle Bob's bunions."

His response was to gobble up the second installment. "Ah," he said, his voice ecstatic. "Ummmmm." But moments later he clutched his stomach. "Ohhhhhh." Now he was moaning in an ecstasy of pain.

"Vesuvius!" cried Henry with all the depth of an innkeeper's wisdom.

Mr. Thackeray erupted from the booth, nearly knocking an astonished Adele off her feet. Stamps flew through the air, twisting and turning like autumn leaves, as they fluttered to the floor.

The man reeled to his left, tilted to his right, and finally staggered to a stop against the wall.

"Yeow!" he cried. He reached down to grasp his ankle.

The nail that had snagged shawls, torn hems, and punctured ankles had once again claimed another victim.

Like a hulking ship in a gale, Mr. Thackeray listed toward the bar.

"Milk!" he cried. "Milk and treacle! They're the only antidotes."

Henry bent down and examined the baseboard. "I'll have to get that nail pulled," he said, echoing the words of every landlord since the time of King Charles the Second.

While all attention was focused on the innkeeper and the ailing Mr. Thackeray, Skilley—as casual as a cat could be—strolled across the floor, paused as if to sniff the floorboards for mice, then slipped, unnoticed, out of the room.

I ought to have been at The Cheese yesterday evening! I curse myself for staying home. It would have made a wonderful scene for a book.

Thackeray was up to his usual gastronomic mischief, and Henry is no match for him. Of all things for men to love so foolishly! I fear dear William will suffer more than the occasional ulcerous spasm of pain as a result of his affection for red peppers.

They will be the death of him yet.

Ah—a baffling side note to last evening's events. Adele, the temperamental barmaid, recounted the strangest anecdote about that extraordinary blue cat. She saw it with "me own two blinkin' eyes!" to quote the girl. She swears the cat ate a stamp! A penny red! He licked it up, she reported, right off the floor and, looking right pleased with himself, sauntered from the room. Perhaps to post himself to—whom?

This gives me an idea for my story of the French Revolution. A letter, written in soot mixed with blood—Yes! Oh my, I must return to it immediately, while my thoughts are still clear.

CHAPTER THIRTY-SEVEN

It is neither an easy nor a welcome task to compose a letter by committee (ask any writer). Particularly when the committee is as full of headstrong, inappropriate, and contradictory opinions as the one that gathered at Ye Olde Cheshire Cheese that evening.

Skilley was included in this delegation, as was Maldwyn. After all, the letter under consideration concerned him most directly.

Pip patiently listened as nearly every member of the committee put forward a proposal—or two or three—for the wording of the message.

"Tell 'em to come quick."

"Tell 'em he's at The Cheese."

"Don't forget to mention those most wicked cats what attacked him."

"And tell 'em to bring fresh meat. Uh, Maldwyn told me to say that."

"I did not!"

"Yes, you did. Just now."

"No, I didn't."

"Then what did you say?"

"Erm, I said... Dash it all!" cursed Maldwyn. "What's wrong with fresh meat? I haven't had any in ages. I'm sick to death of suet."

"And while we're on the subject, what about tellin' 'em to get rid of all mouse traps in London, eh?"

"And..."

"And..."

Pip listened. He secretly discarded the suggestions that had no place in a formal letter to the White Tower, especially those referring to the abolition of mouse traps, hawks, and cats—such requests would only muddle the message.

In the end, Pip knew that it would be up to him to compose the letter. For what was left of the evening, he puzzled over what to say. The following morning he was still mulling over every word, arranging and rearranging until each had found its perfect place.

At last the words were ready to be set to the scrap of brown paper Nudge and Too had wrestled up the stairs and into the garret.

"It's a bit stained," apologized Nudge, "but it was the best we could find."

"Is that blood?" asked Skilley, screwing up his face in disgust.

"It was wrapped about a bit of beef," explained Nudge, "but there's plenty of room left for the words."

"It will have to do," said Pip. "I've already addressed the envelope you took from Henry's desk. I think we have everything we need now."

As a tiny mouse with little more than wits and a tail, he should have felt daunted by the challenge. He had prepared himself, however, for this moment.

Every mouse has a destiny, Pip thought. *Perhaps this is why I was spared on that black day in the onion bin.*

"Pip!" Skilley roused him from his thoughts and spurred him on to the task at hand.

The mouse squared his shoulders. He dipped the tip of his tail in the thimble of India ink, tapped it against the rim, and approached the sheet of paper.

The others watched anxiously.

"Just write the important words," urged Skilley. "And hurry. I'm more worried than ever about Pinch. He's taken to following me about. It may not be long before he comes sniffing up here."

"Let him," squawked Maldwyn. "We'll see how he fares without his cutthroat comrades."

"Hush," said Pip. "Be still now, everyone, while I think." He closed his eyes and pictured the note. In his mind it read thus:

To the Yeoman Warder and Ravenmaster

Esteemed Sir,

The raven Her Majesty believes kidnapped is alive and safe at Ye Olde Cheshire Cheese of Fleet Street, where he recovers from a vicious attack by a band of alley cats. Come alone, as we are afraid a crowd would alarm him.

If possible, bring a few pounds of fresh meat, as he has not had anything but table scraps for a good long while and would pay a king's ransom for some decent victuals.

A thousand thanks in advance,

A Friend

He opened his eyes, dipped his tail once again, tapped it on the edge of the thimble—

"Get on with it, then!" said Skilley.

"Tell them to hurry," squeaked Too.

"And don't forget the part about the fresh meat," nagged Maldwyn.

"And to come alone," whispered Nudge.

"Yes, yes. I'll get to all that." At last Pip began, carefully forming each letter with the appropriate curl or curve or dash or dot, stopping only for the requisite trips to the inkwell.

"Are you done yet?" asked Maldwyn, who had settled himself among some old rags in a corner of the room.

"No. I've only just written the salutation."

"What?" cried Skilley. "We need to finish this while Victoria is still on the throne. Just put down the important parts!"

"You don't understand," explained Pip. "There is more to writing than tossing down a few haphazard words; words must have context."

"Huh?" grunted the three onlookers, followed by Too's high-pitched "Erh?"

"Context. Ummmm…" Pip gave his ear a scratch. "Well, you see, words have to be in the right place in order to have meaning. You need to know where they've been, and where they're going. You wouldn't just eat a piece of cheese without knowing where it's been, would you?"

"I would," said Nudge.

"So would I," added Skilley.

"What about the fresh meat?" cried Maldwyn.

Pip opened his mouth.

Then closed it.

Opened it.

Closed it again.

Lowering his chin to his chest, he released a shudder-
ing sigh and then returned to the note.

"Please," urged Skilley again, "can't you go faster?"

"You could bring the ink closer, if you really wish to
help," said Pip, becoming a bit testy.

"Why are you making the letters so big? Why not the
size they are in the newspaper?"

"Because that's not the way the humans do it, and we
want it to appear authentic. Now let me—"

"I...I...I've got an idea!" shouted Nudge, his face
suddenly convulsed with enthusiasm. After all, from
his dim mind ideas were rare, and therefore all the
more precious. "Why don't we just use the words from
the newspaper? Cut them out. Put them on the page.
Wouldn't that be faster?"

"Uh..." Pip looked longingly at the inkwell, then
glanced back to the inviting sheet of paper.

"That's brilliant!" exclaimed Skilley. "That way we can
all work together. Pip, you choose the words. Maldwyn
can snip them out with his beak—"

"I prefer to use my talons for delicate tasks—"

"Yes, yes. Talons, then," agreed Skilley. "And good
old Nudge and I can put the scraps of paper in place."

"But there's a problem with your clever proposal," Pip
objected. "What's to keep the words on the page?"

"Ummm. Treacle?" suggested Nudge.

Pip shook his head. "Too messy."

"Honey?" said Maldwyn.

"Too sticky. And it would attract flies."

But it was now Skilley's turn for brilliance. The image of Pinch with shredded newspaper stuck to his side flashed into his mind. "A little spit and wheat flour from the kitchen should do the trick," he said.

"Too'll fetch the flour," offered the smallest mouse. "Come, Nudge."

Pip was loath to leave off the writing, as it was so enjoyable. Still, his friends were right to be concerned; it was taking a long time. Despite a nagging misgiving, he gave in to their persuasion.

"All right," he finally conceded. "I'll select the words. Come with me, Maldwyn. Please?"

In his excited state, the raven had no problem obeying the orders from this mouse. *A plan of action, at long last!* It worked as a tonic. Maldwyn was almost spry as he skipped and hobbled after Pip to the pile of newsprint out on the landing.

CHAPTER THIRTY-EIGHT

Pip, nose down and oblivious to all else, scurried over the page, marking each word with an ink-swipe of his tail. While Maldwyn enthusiastically attacked those portions selected, Pip scanned ahead.

Too and Nudge, who had returned with a cloud of flour piled high on an old button, joined the brigade. It became their task to rush the scraps of paper into the garret, where Skilley placed them on the page in the precise order Pip sent them.

Finally, Pip cried, "There! That's the last of it." He peeked through the door. "Wait! You haven't begun pasting them yet, have you?" He rushed around the page. "Oh! You haven't. Good. I'll just do a final reading—"

"Um, Pip?" called a mouse from the top of the stairs. His black eyes were open so wide they made him look rather comical—or alarmed—or both.

"What is it?" asked Pip, suddenly worried.

"It's Nell. She's...here."

Delighted, Pip took to his heels without a backward glance. In his haste, he tore straight across the brown paper on which lay the dozens of words so painstakingly arranged. In his wake, they floated down willy-nilly, like so much lexicographical confetti. As they came to rest on the blood-spattered paper, they found a new (and unintended) order.

But Skilley's disbelief at the startling announcement was crowding out all his other senses. "Nell?" he gulped.

No one answered him.

"Nell?" This time he directed his question at Too.

"Nell." The young mouse sighed. "She was good to Too."

"Was? So she is dea——?"

"You want to see her?"

"NO! Uh, well..." Skilley tried to stifle the alarm in his voice. He had no desire to meet a ghost face-to-face. "Later. Perhaps. We've, er, got to finish this letter. And it looks a mess now, doesn't it?"

This drew everyone's attention to the paper.

"They're all there, aren't they?" snapped Maldwyn, his impatience reaching Olympian heights. "Let's get on with it, then."

Too dutifully emptied the flour onto the floor next to the letter, and Maldwyn was only too eager to provide the spit. Everyone soon got into the spirit of the thing, and before long, the task was completed. Only Skilley showed concern as all gathered around the paper to survey their handi-work.

"Are we sure it still says all those things we discussed?" he asked.

"Close enough, I guess," answered Nudge.

"But what'll we do with the leftover bits?" Too asked, playing with the snippets of newspaper still scattered over the floor.

"Just stick 'em on the page," Nudge said. "Except maybe those little ones. And that one there—I don't like the look of it."

"Oh, just sweep them between the floorboards," squawked Maldwyn. "Who's to know?"

And that's what they did.

Skilley again squinted at the paper, holding a paw over one eye, then the other, trying to extract meaning from the strange black marks. Had he been able, this is what he would have read, perhaps with a sense of misgiving:

"Well," Skilley said. "We'd best put it in the envelope and close it up. Do we have enough flour to paste it shut?"

"No, no," Maldwyn said. "It must be done properly. I've seen the Ravenmaster do this often enough. Bring the candle closer."

"The candle?" asked Skilley.

"He's gonna burn it!" cried Too, tugging at her ears. But the raven had no intention of burning the letter that was to be the instrument of his salvation. Instead, he lifted the candle with his claw and tilted it just enough to drip a small mound of wax onto the flap of the envelope.

"Hold it closed!" he commanded.

While the wax was still warm and yield-ing, he firmly pressed his claw into its center.

"There," he said. "Now let's get it to the post!"

Tower RAVEN KIDNAPPED alive safe at CHESHIRE Cheese Come alone afraid thousand pounds ransom in ADVANCE or meat vicious band

155

CHAPTER THIRTY-NINE

"What the—?" Skilley's fur rose along his back like hedgehog quills. Too confirmed Skilley's worst fears with a single cry, "Nell!"

The girl was framed in the garret doorway, the setting sun shining brightly through a dormer window behind her. For a moment, Skilley was hypnotized by the golden vision. Then—as stalwart a fellow as he was proving to be—he nonetheless gave in to a most unheroic faint.

CHAPTER FORTY

"Cat? Cat!" There was a desperate concern in the voice that pulled Skilley from his swoon. As he regained consciousness, he realized it was no ghostly figure that summoned him. Skilley looked up into Nell's face. To his expanding relief it was made up entirely of flesh and blood.

"Pip!" the girl exclaimed. "He's come 'round at last."

Pip scuttled close to Skilley. The mouse's nose wriggled and twitched. "Oh, dear," he whispered, furrowing his brow. "Whatever overcame you?"

"N-Nell." Skilley nearly choked on the name, not quite as recovered as he thought.

"Yes, this is Nell."

"I thought she was dead," Skilley said.

"Dead? Why Nell's not dead, she's been living in Chessington. You thought..." The corner of Pip's mouth quivered, and his prodigious teeth made concealing the grin out of the question.

"But you said she was..."

"I'm sure I never did..." Pip shook his head so vigorously his ears made a soft flapping sound.

"If she wasn't…isn't…dead," demanded an adamant Skilley, "then what about the tears, and all that 'poor Nell' business each time the girl's name was mentioned?"

"Poor Nell she is." Pip's tone was mirthless now. "She's been banished, sent to live with her aunt in the country and only allowed home for short visits. Henry is convinced that being at the inn will provoke another crisis of nerves." Pip's voice was a whisper, as though he feared Nell might hear and comprehend. "They think she's barmy."

"Well, is she? Is she barmy?" Skilley found himself whispering back. All this, of course, sounded like nothing more than purring and twittering to Nell, who by now had turned her attention to the ailing Maldwyn.

"Indeed she is not!" Pip was indignant. "She simply confided a secret, you see, to the wrong person."

"Secret?"

"She told Adele about me."

Skilley glanced at the girl. "And then?" This was not at all the story he'd expected.

"Well, Adele told Croomes, and Croomes told Henry, and Henry consulted two physicians and a midwife's sister-in-law. Their collective advice was to send her forthwith to the country for a rest cure. A rest cure, mind you. To an aunt with ten children and no governess. But you'll never hear Nell complain. Our Nell's a—"

We are never to know what heights the girl might have attained in Pip's estimation for he stopped mid-sentence when his eye fell on the envelope lying but a few feet away.

"You sealed the letter? Oh, dear me, I would have preferred to read through it once—"

"Oh, we did. I mean, it's all there. Just like you instructed." Skilley didn't mention the scraps that had been swept beneath the floor. It would just worry Pip, and his new friend already indulged in enough fretful washing and grooming.

Having nestled Maldwyn in a corner with a bit of sugar she produced from her apron pocket, Nell settled to the floor. She invited the two animals onto her lap. "The pair of you seems to be getting along quite nicely." She touched Pip's nose with a light finger. "Trust you, Pip, to tame a cat."

Skilley squinted up at the girl, not altogether pleased with her assessment of the situation.

Nell shifted her legs to a more comfortable position. "Now what's this?"

She reached for the letter with its crimson stamp and the address Pip had so painstakingly penned earlier that day. This caused Pip to grow quite agitated.

"What are you chattering on about, Pip?"

In answer, the mouse abandoned her lap and crossed

the floor to the thimble of ink. He dipped his tail and hurried back to Nell.

She stretched out her hand as was their habit, and Pip wrote across her palm,

$$\text{MINE.}$$

"Is it, now?" Nell raised her brows in mock surprise. "I knew I'd regret teaching you your letters."

Pip chattered in protest.

"No, no. I *am* proud of you. But what's this? You've sealed it." She inspected the envelope closely, then turned her attention to the raven. "You've had a hand—um, talon—in this, too, I see. Now, I'm more than a trifle tempted to steal a peek." She tapped the letter against her chin.

This suggestion was met with more emphatic chittering.

"I surrender! After all, a mouse that can read *and* write must have good reason to send a letter to"—she read the address out loud—"The Tower of London?" Now she halted. "Pip, are you sure of what you're doing?"

Pip wished he could explain it all to her in human talk; instead, he scrambled to her other hand and scrawled a second word. This one was a request.

POST?

You want me to post this for you?" Her forehead wrinkled in an expression of mild worry.

Pip wrapped his tail around her finger and gave her an imploring look.

"Very well," she sighed. "I don't suppose much harm could come from it." And so it was that another gatekeeper allowed the letter to continue its journey unchecked.

Maldwyn gave a soft ravenly grunt of relief. He had abandoned his nest of comfortable rags to rest himself against Nell's leg. She stroked the smooth feathers between his eyes, and he didn't snap at her.

She's sweet, this one, Skilley thought as she scratched behind his left ear, *but she's odd, even for a human.* Then he did what all cats do under similar circumstances. He yawned and stretched and flexed his claws oh so carefully...

His drowsy gaze passed over the top of the stairs.

Pinch was there.

And then he vanished.

"What in the name of heaven was that?" asked Nell.

"He's seen Maldwyn," Skilley hissed to Pip.

A hurried trip back to the thimble of ink.

Another scribble. This time on the back of her hand.

Nell read it aloud as she scrambled to her feet.

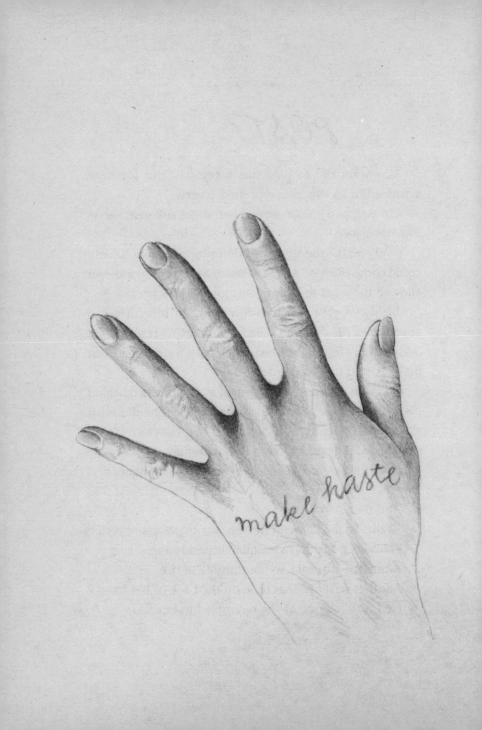

CHAPTER FORTY-ONE

The next day, Nell stood in the hallway alongside her traveling trunk, looking forlorn. She lifted Pip out of her pocket.

"So it's farewell, again, dear Pip."

Pip wiped his eyes. The fur along his snout was damp
from tears.

"I scarcely slept from worry about all of you." Nell bit
her lip and looked about the hallway before continuing.
"My auntie's house is so far away and the raven's wing is
healing poorly. Then there's that ginger cat of Adele's; he
is a devil, I'm sure of it. Stay clear of him. *Promise me, Pip.*"

Pip gave Nell a reassuring squeak just as her father
appeared. The mouse instantly retreated into Nell's pocket.
When the innkeeper pulled his daughter into a tight bear
hug, Pip curled into a tiny ball, fearful of being crushed.

"My dearest Nell," Henry said in a sad tone that
showed more of his fatherly concern than words could
convey. "Get better soon and return to us in good health.
This place is much too dull without you."

The girl stretched her own arms about her rotund
father, then pulled away and looked him in the eyes.

"I am better, Papa. I was never unwell. If only you would believe me. Pip really *can* communicate—"

"Of course he can. I believe you." These unlikely words of solidarity came from Croomes. So surprising was this statement from the cook that Pip risked poking the top of his head out of Nell's pocket.

Adele stood silently at the larger woman's side.

The cook handed Nell something wrapped in a napkin and added, "This here's some victuals for your journey, miss. I'm that sorry for the trouble I caused you." With an uncharacteristic dab at her eyes, she turned away.

As Croomes passed Henry, she muttered, "You cold-hearted oafstool." She elbowed Adele aside and shambled back toward her kitchen, her broad shoulders drooping.

It was Adele's turn to embrace the girl. "You'll be yerself soon, miss. Small wonder you think them mouses is talkin' to you, with 'em overrunnin' the place. Sometimes I think I hear 'em meself. Ne'er you mind. It's a new game now that me Oliver is 'ere, innit?"

Nell stiffened, then shook herself out of the barmaid's arms. Her naturally cheerful and radiant face took on a dark look. "Father." Her voice was firm. "I will not be returning to Auntie's. I'm going upstairs to unpack my things." The usual warmth in her voice was absent.

Everyone began to speak at once, and Croomes, who had been halfway down the stairs when she heard Nell's glorious rebellion, swiveled and took the steps back up to the hallway with a vengeance.

"You're staying, then?" Her face split into a smile, all gums and teeth.

"She is not staying," said Henry.

"Father—"

"I will not be gainsaid," growled Henry.

"But Father…"

Henry's eyes unwillingly met Nell's. His gaze was held by a stubborn look so familiar that it broke his heart.

"You can send me back for a month or a year, Father. Sane or mad, I am what I am. I have been a terrible trial to Aunt Edith and I must confess that I was not a good guest while under her roof.

"I unrepentantly continued my rescue

Nell

of unfortunate creatures. The day she discovered the snake in her chamber pot, she confined herself to bed for a week.

"So you see, dearest Father, it would be most unfair of you to continue to press upon your sister a child that is as unchangeable and unremorseful as your Nell."

"You," said Henry, leaning forward and tapping her on the forehead, "are just like your mother."

"And it's high time you recognized it, too," said Croomes.

Adele

It was Adele, however, who had the last words on the matter.

No one heard them but Skilley. While everyone else was helping Nell settle back into her room upstairs, he wandered into the kitchen looking for scraps. There he found the barmaid in a rather one-sided conversation with a cleaver.

"Me auntie indeed! I saw right through that 'oodwink. She means to save 'er chatterin' mice. Talk, dance—I don't care if they can cure the pox, they're filthy mouses, and now Croomes 'as gone soft for 'em, too. But you 'aven't gone soft, 'ave you, my pet? " she cooed, addressing the cleaver in her hand. Then, with a single swing of the newly sharpened blade, she savaged a perfectly blameless cabbage.

"They're cooking up something particularly nasty," Skilley said. "I'm sure of it."

"They?" asked Pip.

"They," Skilley answered. "Pinch and Adele."

"That's absurd! Adele?"

"Aye, Adele. That girl's not right. You should have seen her swing that cleaver. And now that Pinch knows of Maldwyn, the raven is in as much danger as the day he fell out of the sky. I know Pinch, and he will be determined to finish what he started that day in the alley; he won't be satisfied until he tastes Maldwyn's blood."

"Well, we've already decided we can't move him," Pip

said. "He's too feeble. Besides, Nell has managed to block the door with an old chest from the attic."

Still, Skilley's streetwise sense of danger, that sixth sense that judged every situation by calculating risk, chillingly placed the odds in Pinch's favor.

I attempt to write. Yet each day my thoughts drift further and further from my own tale. I am now consumed with curiosity about the comings and goings of the animals of this inn. I feel as if some great mischief were about to befall them all.

Nevertheless, there is good news. Nell's unjust banishment has ended, and her presence lightens the air in this place.

Still, I despair. The deadline for my first issue of ALL THE YEAR ROUND looms and as yet I have no opening line...

The ginger cat has just crept from behind the chop house drapery and appears to be shadowing the blue—

No! I must, must, attend to my own work today.

CHAPTER FORTY-TWO

What happened next in the inn took Pip and Skilley by surprise.

Nothing.

At.

All.

At least nothing out of the ordinary and certainly not the thing that Pip had hoped for.

The letter had been posted.

Nell had decided to stay.

Adele and Pinch continued their unholy confederacy.

And still the Ravenmaster did not come.

He did not come after one day.

He did not come after three days.

He did not come after a whole week of days.

If they hadn't entrusted the letter to Nell, they would have feared the task had been bungled.

In his impatience Pip took to stationing himself within the fronds of a potted palm near the chop room window. From this post he watched and waited for the arrival of a carriage bearing the emblem of the White Tower.

Mr. Dickens kept him company, taking his usual seat by that same window, his notebook always open and his pen in hand as if expecting some brilliant notion to strike him at any moment. And yet, he wrote little. At times he walked the inn, looking first in one room and then in another. Twice Croomes removed him from the kitchen.

By the end of that week, the only truly unusual occurrence Pip had witnessed was the arrival of a stranger.

That in itself wasn't so very unusual, as strangers often came to the inn. But this man wore a heavy cloak and a drover's hat pulled down to cover his face. That, too, wasn't unusual—it was, after all, still winter, and a cold rain rattled through the streets, gusting sheets of frigid water throughout the storm-tossed city.

What was unusual was that the man didn't remove his hat and cloak. He did not uncover his face. He did not seek a seat close to the fire. Rather, he settled himself in the corner and slouched down into an unmoving lump, not even ordering a pint when Nell offered.

She glanced at Mr. Dickens. Catching his gaze, she cocked her head in the direction of the stranger as if to ask, "What do you make of 'im?"

Dickens answered with an indifferent shrug, but his eyes, bright with curiosity, told a different story.

Pip turned his attention to the goings-on outside of

the inn. This was good, as otherwise he would have missed the shuttered carriage that rattled to a stop in front of Ye Olde Cheshire Cheese. Its swaying gradually subsided, but no one disembarked. Its driver huddled beneath his oilskin, proof against the driving rain.

Pip glanced back and forth between the stranger in the room and the carriage outside. There was something suspicious in the attitude of both (if a carriage could adopt an attitude).

Pip shivered, partly with the wet and dreary cold, and partly from premonition.

CHAPTER FORTY-THREE

What happened next is difficult to relate, and even more difficult to believe for those who did not witness the strange happenings that day. It was as if the devil's own lieutenant had broken loose and spread chaos throughout the Cheese.

As volcanic events often do, however, they began with only a rumble.

A rumble named Adele.

While Pip stared out the window, his interest in the carriage flagging, he witnessed a bundled-up Adele scurrying toward him through the stinging rain, a brown-paper parcel clutched to her chest. She'd been off to fetch Henry's shirts from the laundress (and also to visit a certain coal man along the way, else why brave the storm for a few clean shirts?).

She slowed as she neared that very carriage, and stopped to look up at the sodden driver. Ever the snoop, she tried to peek in a shuttered window. Without warning, the driver came to life and snapped his whip at her.

She yelled something up to the man that Pip couldn't quite make out; in response, the driver's eyes widened and his jaw loosened, which caused him to drop the stub of a cigar he'd had clutched in his teeth. She left him hacking and wiping his trousers.

Adele burst into the chop room. "What's all that, then?" she cried. "Imagine, a fine carriage such as that outside the Cheese?" She dropped the parcel on a table and shook off her cloak, scattering rainwater upon the sawdust and wooden planks.

"You'd better mop that up," demanded Henry. "Someone's sure to take a tumble."

"But, 'oo d'you think is in the carriage, eh?"

"What do I care for carriages that bring me no business?" Henry snapped. The weather was making him cross, which didn't help Adele's mood either.

She picked up the parcel of shirts and flung it at the landlord's head. "Get yer own shirts next time, then! I's only curious."

At last, the figure in the corner raised his head to speak. "It's no one," he said. "Don't mind the carriage." He stood and strode to the window by Mr. Dickens's table. "Pardon me, sir." His cloak brushed the writer's leg as he looked out past Pip and the potted plant.

"Certainly," said Mr. Dickens. "A fine day for a ride in the city, isn't it?" His voice suggested the contrary.

The man ignored Mr. Dickens's sarcasm; rather, responding to some unimaginable sight outside, he released a half-whispered oath. This was followed by a cry—"No! She wouldn't!"—and a headlong dash toward the pub's entrance.

Adele joined Mr. Dickens, and they looked to the street. Pip peered between the fronds of the palm.

The carriage door opened, and out stepped a short, stout woman, a gauzy veil covering her face. She was followed by several gentlemen arrayed in traveling cloaks and beaver hats—very stiff-looking gentlemen who followed the woman as if attached by an invisible thread. Last to emerge was a squat man with a wild wisp of gray hair that stood up from his bare head and refused to give in to the drenching rain.

This gentleman scurried before the woman, begging, entreating, his gestures expressing clear exasperation. The woman turned her face to his and stopped all further protests with a single withering glance. She then redirected the glance, and herself, to the inn's door.

Her humbled entourage followed.

With great curiosity, Adele rushed toward that door, too, but she slipped in the puddle of rainwater she herself had brought in with her cloak. Her feet shot up above her shoulders, her skirt flew over her head, and she landed on her bottom with a thump and a curse and a clattering of coins that spilled from her pocket. The stranger in the slouch hat, backing away from the new arrivals, tripped over Adele. He fell sprawling to the floor, losing the hat and much of his dignity in the process.

The woman from the carriage stood over the two figures at her feet. "My dear," she said to Adele, "is that the proper way to welcome guests?"

"I—oh—beggin' yer pardon, mum." With a frantic hand she scrabbled to gather up the coins. "I am, as you can see, a...a...fallen woman." Adele's innocent reply brought the room to a standstill. Mr. Dickens turned to inspect a portrait he seemed to find suddenly quite captivating.

The lady addressed Adele. Her words were as carefully chosen as the young woman's had been slapdash. The voice held a mixture of reproof and, possibly, of humor. "It would be wise in future, my child, to place your words more judiciously than you have your foot; a woman who has fallen must never be mistaken for a fallen woman."

A stifled snort was heard from Dickens.

The visitor turned to the man on the floor. "We tired of waiting."

He scrambled to his feet. "B-B-But I haven't yet secured your safety."

Meanwhile, Mr. Dickens crossed the room and offered a hand to Adele. With a guilty glance toward Henry, she deftly shoved the coins back into her pocket before rising.

Mr. Dickens turned to the woman visitor and bowed.

"Good afternoon, Your Majesty. What brings you to Ye Olde Cheshire Cheese on such an intemperate day as this?"

Queen Victoria

CHAPTER FORTY-FOUR

Behind the veil, Queen Victoria's voice momentarily warmed in recognition and surprise.

"Mr. Dickens, is it not? If We recall you properly, that is, from your brilliant performance before Our Person."

This time, Dickens gave the deepest, most elegant bow of his life. "Welcome to the finest inn in the realm, Your Majesty."

The lady, remembering her purpose, had a quick and hot retort: "And the hiding place of a jewel of that self-same realm—which belongs to Us. A jewel that was stolen by brigands and is even now being held for ransom." She paused. Impatiently waving aside offers of aid, she removed her veil. "There'll be no more need of this." Divested of her head covering, she appeared for all the company as the beloved and familiar face on the penny red stamp.

Adele whimpered.

Mr. Dickens rescued her elbow, along with the rest of the girl, who managed a poorly executed half curtsey before she turned on her heel and raced from the room.

Pip could hear her cries fading as she descended the stairs toward the kitchen.

The Queen watched the barmaid go with a frown of disapproval—after all, the girl had not been given leave to depart the Royal Presence. But, fortunately for Adele, the Queen had weightier concerns at present. She turned her royal attention back to the remaining occupants of the room.

Her Majesty.

The words sank into Pip's whirligig of a brain.

But, wait! Did she say jewel?

What *jewel?*

Good heavens, was she speaking of Maldwyn?

And what was that about a…a *ransom?*

CHAPTER FORTY-FIVE

Unaware of the scene being played out in the chop room, Skilley was ascending the cellar stairs when he heard a rumbling tread on the steps above. Silent as only a cat can be, he backed away into the cellar's gloom and hid himself beside a cask of claret.

Croomes's heavy foot nearly crushed his tail as she passed. Skilley retreated further into the shadows. The cook was muttering to herself and he caught a fragment of her soliloquy.

"I'll not have it, I won't! Rid The Cheese of every mouse, she says? And, then what? Bring down ruin and penury on all our heads? Rattlebrained girl! I'll have to do something about that Adele…"

Skilley listened, confused. What was the cook going on about now? It's true, Croomes had been in a fretful mood of late. She had taken to accusing thieves of being in the larders. Thieves, mind you, who had no interest in pewter or lockets or Henry's silver. Only cheese. Still, she had realized the folly of blaming the cats. And since the mice only took their portion—as ever they had—she concluded there must be a band of robbers on the loose bent on pinching her legendary Cheshire.

Even muddleheaded Henry had balked at this theory. "Cheese thieves, you say?" The question was followed by a snort.

"Ay, I do say!" was the cook's scalding retort. "And when I nab 'em, I'll give each and every one a good roasting!"

Oh, she had her suspicions, and they had festered.

She had confided them to Skilley one day while holding him up by the scruff of the neck. Each theory she proposed was punctuated with a vigorous shake. Young Jack, the potboy, certainly had the heavy brow of a criminal, she'd said. And Gertie, the under cook, had expanded about the waist as if she had taken on a richer diet of late.

"Chuzzlewitted clodpates!" she'd ranted. "They've no respect for an artist. Me cheese is the finest in London, ain't it? And a few cheese-stealing mice I don't mind, do I?" Here her gaze had bored into Skilley, and she'd sniffed at his whiskers. "Nor a strange cat like you, eh? I let 'em have their bit of cheese, and in their turn them grateful mice—" But she'd bitten off the end of the peculiar statement before Skilley could learn what it was the mice did for Croomes in their turn. And what had she meant about him? Could she possibly have guessed?

This inn has more secrets than mice, he thought.

Skilley returned to the present when he heard the rattle of keys…and the click of a lock.

He peeked 'round the wine cask.

The door to the cheese room swung open under Croomes's hand, and then the turgid cook shuffled inside. The light from her candle faded to a weak glow.

Out drifted the mouthwatering aroma of Cheshire cheese.

Skilley's nose twitched. *If only she would leave the door open when she comes out*, he thought.

A minute passed.

"Cook!" A breathless Adele, hair loosened from its pins, came down the stair steps two at a time. "Come quick!"

Croomes emerged carrying a round of cheese under her arm. "Egad, girl!" growled the mountain of a woman. "You've about startled me out of me pantaloons. Collect yourself."

"But, Cook, only come quick. Someone's 'ere. And you'll never guess. Not in a 'undred 'undred years!"

She bent close and whispered words that Skilley couldn't make out.

Croomes nearly lost her grip on the round of Cheshire cheese. "You're jesting!"

"It's true, mum! I swear it!" Adele cried.

Croomes must have believed her, for she lurched toward the stairs with a quickness one would have thought impossible in a being of her age and lumpish form.

Adele followed close on her heels.

Skilley watched them disappear, then glanced at the dim light coming from the open and welcoming cheese-room door.

He hesitated, his eyes on the steps.

One minute.

Two.

Satisfied that they were not coming back, Skilley crept from his hiding place, sniffing the air. A fragrance like incense filled the room, from the stone slabs to the arched ceiling.

Ah! Cheeeeeeeese.

Its pungent aroma beckoned him through the open door. He paused for a half breath, then softly padded inside.

CHAPTER FORTY-SIX

Skilley stared openmouthed at the shelves and tables stacked high with wheel upon wheel of Cheshire cheese. On the other side of the room, old door panels lying across trestles bowed under the weight of their golden burdens.

Gro-o-o-o-an.

Slam!

Skilley spun toward the firmly latched door.

"Who's out there?" he demanded.

He was answered by a spiteful voice. "Never mind who's out 'ere. It's you who's in there, eh? And it's your friends who'll pay dear for it. That dimwitted barmaid 'as moved a certain chest back from a partic'lar door. An' what d'you suppose she found? But don't worry. She left 'im for me. But smaller matters first."

Driven by anger and fear, Skilley dashed himself against the unyielding oak planks.

I hate doors!

He paced. He growled. He spat.

It was a carelessly slammed door that had made of his

tail a useless hook. Yet that hapless moment had never been the true reason for his loathing.

Bitter memories are like things behind locked doors, thought Skilley. *Dark things that rattle the door handles, whisper your name through the keyholes, and tear at the wood with their fingernails. They want to be released to do their terrible work: the work of making you remember things best left forgotten.*

When Skilley's hidden memories burst through their restraints, they paralyzed his mind with fear. He gave in to a loosening of his limbs and slid to the floor. As the darkness pressed in on him, Skilley remembered his first friend.

The boy was much thinner than the others at the workhouse, but he was tall. His fingers could just reach the half-starved kitten mewing on the frozen windowsill of their dormitory. The boy had hidden the shivering animal in his grimy nightshirt and climbed onto his threadbare pallet, where they had warmed one another until morning. He had named the kitten Skilley, after the thin porridge the two shared, scarcely

enough food for one. The child kept them from starving with crusts of bread and bits of cheese he stole from the kitchen. Boy and kitten were never apart; for two blissful weeks Skilley lived, undetected, inside the boy's shirt.

Until the night the child was caught thieving cheese.

And Skilley was discovered.

Skilley could still hear the boy's wails and protests as he was torn from his arms and flung onto the street. He could still see the door that had cost him his only friend. No! Not his only friend—

Pip!

Skilley's eyes snapped open.

CHAPTER FORTY-SEVEN

"Majesty, I'm sure there's no such skullduggery as that here at The Cheese. And certainly no brigands nor jewels," said Henry with a fawning bow. The astonishing events of the past half hour had left him mute 'til now.

Nonetheless, he was to prove himself an innkeeper, through and through. "But we are well-known for our excellent cheese. If Your Majesty and your party would care to take a table...perhaps upstairs in a private room?"

"We, sir, are not here for the cheese. We are here for the raven." The voice, regal in its use of plural pronouns, caused Henry to shrink back a step.

"Raven? Oh, dear. We don't serve raven. But, if—"

"No, no, no." The Queen closed her eyes; this gesture was accompanied by an almost inaudible moan.

"Silence!" the man in the cloak barked at Henry.

Oh dear, Pip thought.

While all attention was focused on Queen Victoria, as befitted her station and the strange occasion, Pip crept from the potted palm, scurried across the table, and dropped to the floor. He drew a deep breath before he darted toward a hole in the far wall. Just before he reached that safety, he heard an imperious query:

"Is that a mouse?"

CHAPTER FORTY-EIGHT

Skilley, imprisoned with the most glorious cheese in all of England, had lost his appetite.

Once he regained control of his senses, he charged the door repeatedly, but in vain. He jumped shelves and tables, searched the walls, and inspected the beams and stone. There seemed to be countless crevices and cracks, but none big enough for a cat to squeeze through.

"Pip!" he cried at each hole. "Nudge! Too! Anyone!" *Please, someone answer.*

Frantic, he once again flung himself at the recalcitrant door, but the infernal thing would only obey the latch.

"Uh, Skilley, sir?"

It was Nudge. He'd crept down through the ceiling and was sitting on a shelf, smoothing his whiskers with a paw.

Skilley could hear a soft smacking sound. Was the fellow ...eating?

Though Croomes's stub of a candle had burned itself out, leaving only the ribbon of light beneath the door, Skilley had little difficulty piercing the darkness with his cat's eyes.

"I heard you calling." More chewing. "Did you get hold of Cook's keys, then? Darned clever of you."

"I did not get hold of Cook's keys," Skilley snapped. Really, when these mice tasted cheese they seemed to lose all reason. "I'm trapped and Pinch has something foul in mind! You must warn Pip—fly, Nudge, fly!"

Croomes and Adele reached the chop room in time to hear the Queen's cry: *Is that a mouse?*

With no other weapon at hand, Adele wrenched the round of cheese from Croomes's grasp and hurled it at Pip. It split against the floorboard and knocked Pip through the mouse hole. He hit the inside wall with enough force to send him bouncing back out of the hole and onto the floor, where he lay stunned for a second.

"Get 'im!" he heard Adele cry, followed by other shouts, and amidst the chaos, the snarl of a cat.

Pip dashed to the wall, missed the hole, and banged his head again. He felt something grab his paw and yank him into the hole to safety. On the heels of this swift deliverance there came a weighty thump, as the pursuing cat hit the wood paneling.

"Is Pip all right?" It was Too.

He shook his head.

"You're not?"

He shook his head again.

"You are?"

"N-no. Yes. Just a bit woozy. There's something important—but what? Oh, my, I must rally my faculties." Pip cradled his throbbing head with both paws. "Merciful heavens!" The head shot up. "We must go to him right away!"

"Him? Him who?"

"Maldwyn, my dearest Too. We must fetch him from the garret and take him to the Queen—and there's not a moment to lose."

But, in truth, that moment was already lost. A practiced claw reached through the small opening and made a deft swipe.

"Pip!" wailed Too.

CHAPTER FORTY-NINE

Captured!

But how?

Speculation was useless. The fact remained that he was securely and painfully clinched between Pinch's powerful jaws.

Having accustomed himself to traveling in a cat's mouth, the familiarity of it might have been a consolation. But this foul-smelling chamber did not belong to Skilley. And Pip had no doubt that, unpleasant as it was, it would soon be worse—Pinch's mouth would become an abattoir of blood, bone, and guts that would bear testament to his own gruesome end.

Pip felt himself sliding down the rough surface of the cat's tongue, and then he landed on the stone floor with a thud. He scrambled to his feet and tried to run, but made no progress. He looked over his shoulder and saw that Pinch had a front paw firmly on his tail.

"I'm onto the unnatural dealin's 'tween you and that one what calls himself a cat."

He lifted his paw, but the moment Pip began to run, the cat gave him a cruel swat and sent him tumbling into the wall.

"I couldn't believe my eyes when I seen 'im with that bird." Pinch clamped the mouse's tail in his teeth and gave Pip a good shaking, then let go, propelling the little creature across the hallway.

Pip attempted once again to scramble away, but the cat snatched him up, bit down hard, then lunged down the stairs.

Pip winced with pain.

You must get loose, Pip. Once he gets you alone...

Pip began to struggle against Pinch's hold, kicking at the cat's front teeth with his hind legs, scratching at the roof of his mouth with his front claws, but the cat only bit down harder, viciously pinning one of Pip's legs with his front incisor. As the tooth lanced his thigh, Pip felt a radiating agony, followed by a blackening of his senses.

≈

He was just coming to when Pinch released him.

And Pip realized he was falling.

His flailing limbs found nothing more substantial than air to grasp as his eyes briefly met those of his tormentor.

An instant later the world was warm and wet and muffled.

He was under water.

CHAPTER FIFTY

No doubt, that cursed crow thought he was safe here.

Pinch savored the notion as he crouched in the doorway of the garret. His hungry eyes devoured the darkness in search of his prey. They locked on the raven, partly hidden within his nest of rags. A cold, flinty eye stared back, unblinking.

Maldwyn had been expecting him ever since he'd heard Adele drag away the chest. Never one to underestimate an enemy, the raven had understood the calamitous situation from the onset. If he was frightened, he did not seem so.

"You don't belong here," he said. His tone was dismissive.

Pinch responded by drawing closer.

"Do you know who I am?" croaked Maldwyn. It was more threat than question.

At that, Pinch paced back and forth at a respectful distance from the bird. His tail snapped in rhythm to each step. "I never forget an unfinished meal," he spat. "And I know you 'ave a friend in that coward, Skilley."

"Ah, that's where you are wrong. Skilley is no coward. Cowards choose victims, not equals. But they should take care when they choose lest they pick a quarrel with their betters, as you and your friends no doubt discovered that night in the alley. That's my mark across your brow, is it not?"

"Shut your creaky gob!" Pinch took a step nearer.

"If you think me defenseless, your memory is duller than your wit." Maldwyn tottered to his feet and clacked his sharp beak. "Come. Draw closer, if you dare."

Pinch accepted his invitation.

The game was on.

CHAPTER FIFTY-ONE

Water.

He thinks to drown me in a bucket of water!

Pip permitted himself to sink gently out of sight. Despite the throbbing of his injured leg, it took immense effort to keep from smiling.

Brainless cat.

Doesn't he know mice can swim?

Mice can do more than swim. A mouse can hold his breath under water for minutes at a time. Pip exhaled a small stream of bubbles and waited. The water was warm and soothing to his injured leg.

But wait.

Warm water?

Pip arrested his descent. Turning, he paddled furiously upward. When he broke the surface, he found himself encircled by an unbroken wall of iron: Pinch had cast him into one of Croomes's cooking pots.

And judging by the temperature of the water, it would soon simmer, and then...?

No, best not to think that far ahead.

Wasting little time, he swam along the sides of the blackened pot, but try as he might, he could find no imperfection along its curved surface, no friendly dent to which he could grab hold.

His wounded leg pulsed with pain. It was then he noticed the scarlet thread of blood forming a long trail behind him. His breath came in shallow gasps now.

Just stay afloat.

Someone will surely find you.

Steam began to rise around him in wraithlike wisps. Pip cautiously tested the side of the pot. He jerked back his seared paw and tried to hold down the rising panic.

The iron had grown too hot to touch.

CHAPTER FIFTY-TWO

"Skilley!"

"Too! Thank heaven."

"No, thank Nudge. He told me you were down here eatin' cheese. But Skilley-cat!" she cried as she clambered down from one shelf to another. "Pip needs you! Come quick, h-h-he's…he's—"

"He's what? What is it?" Skilley asked.

But he knew.

"What's Pinch done?"

"Cookeded Pip!"

"Cooked him?"

She scurried across the floor and pulled at Skilley's paw. "Skilley-cat must save Pip. Oh, do come! He'll soon be drownded. Or boileded…"

"How? Where?"

"In Cook's pot! Where else would he get boileded?" she asked in exasperation.

Too's panic seemed to be getting the better of her. Her words hardly made sense.

"Stay calm, Too," Skilley said, although he felt a rising

agitation as he grasped the dire nature of her news. Once more he threw himself against the door.

"I'm trapped, can't you see! I'm too large—"

In answer, Too wriggled through the narrow space beneath the door.

What the—? Skilley heard a rattling bounce. Standing on his hind legs, front paws against the door, he tried to peek through the keyhole, but it was no good.

"What are you doing?"

"Too…trying…spring…latch…" She paused to take a deep breath. "Grrrr. Too not heavy enough. Wait here."

Wait? "Too? Please hurry."

CHAPTER FIFTY-THREE

Sweltering heat.

Heat that made him feel like his blood, too, was in danger of boiling.

Too hot…to struggle.

So easy…to let go.

His body growing weaker, Pip's mind flitted like a honeybee from thought to thought.

Maldwyn? What would become of him now?

And Skilley. He should have told him…something…but he could not remember what.

CHAPTER FIFTY-FOUR

Beyond all expectation, the cheese-room door swung open.

Skilley stared in openmouthed wonder at little Too, who raced forward and tugged at his paw.

"Hurry!" she urged.

Then he saw the figure just outside the door, hand still on the latch.

"And how did you get yourself locked in the cheese room?" Nell asked Skilley. She leaned down to address Too. "Is this what had you so upset?"

Too began to chitter as Nell lowered herself onto one knee.

Skilley didn't wait to hear whether Too made herself understood. There wasn't time.

He raced up the stairs toward the kitchen, and Pip.

At the swinging door, a burst of noise from high above stopped him.

"Now, what could that be?" Skilley wondered aloud. But he knew the answer.

Maldwyn. And Pinch.

Skilley did not need to consider the choice before him. He knew without a moment of doubt where his loyalty lay, where it would always lie. Turning his back on the terrible howls and squawks echoing from above, he hurled himself through the kitchen door.

"I'm coming, Pip!" he cried.

CHAPTER FIFTY-FIVE

In two bounds Skilley was atop the chopping-block table that stood next to Cook's stove.

"Pip, are you all right?" he called.

Silence was the heart-wrenching answer.

Skilley stepped on the stove.

"Yeow!" He snatched back his left forefoot and tried to lick the burn out of it.

Despite the pain, he lunged at the lip of the pot with his other paw. Hot, too. Hot, but bearable, though not for long. With his hind legs braced on the wooden table, he pulled at the vessel. It teetered precariously, threatening to spill its contents onto the red-hot surface of the stove. That would not do. He stretched himself as far as he could. It was just enough to peek inside. Pip's nose barely broke the surface of the steaming water; the slow paddling of his paws was hardly perceptible.

Again the heat forced Skilley to pull back.

He searched about. The walls. The floor. The ceiling overhead.

Then he saw them.

Mr. Thackeray's peppers.

They hung in a garland on a hook above the stove. Skilley leapt.

His front paws clawed through the peppers and caught in the bit of rope that held them in place. He swung perilously above the steaming pot.

"My tail!" he cried to Pip, praying it was long enough. "Grab hold of my tail!"

He lowered the offered appendage into the pot, inching himself down, further, further, further. The vapors from the shredded peppers made his eyes smart. He squinched them closed.

He felt nothing but a scalding sensation in his tail.

"Pip! Grab hold!" He swished his tail about in search of the weakening mouse.

"Pip!"

At last Skilley felt the faintest of tugs.

"Hold on!"

He blessed the Fates. It was the unnatural hook of his tail that allowed Skilley to scoop the mouse to safety.

Pip's terror was such that he did not immediately release his feeble grasp on Skilley, even after he was laid on the flagstones: He panted and trembled as his small body cooled.

"Skilley…" This was followed by a fit of coughing.

"Easy, Pip," said Skilley.

"I-I…," Pip sputtered. "Forgive me…"

"Forgive you? Whatever for?"

"For…for not forgiving you."

"Oh, Pip."

"There you are!" a breathless Nell cried. "I've been looking for—oh, dear." With a quick glance at the steaming pot and Pip lying in a soggy heap, Nell's eyes narrowed with anger and comprehension.

"That horrid cat did this, didn't he?" she exclaimed, gathering the mouse up in her gentle hands.

Now that Pip was safe, Skilley looked about for the smaller mouse.

"Where's Too?"

CHAPTER FIFTY-SIX

"Too! No!" squarked Maldwyn.

But Too was determined to avenge Pip. "Wicked, wicked beastie!" she cried as she raced across the floor toward Pinch. With a flying leap, she landed on the cat's tail.

Pinch stared back at her with a glint of amusement. He twitched his tail once, as if to flick her away. But she had a tight hold. And when she parted the fur and clamped her teeth down onto his tender flesh with all her might, he yowled in pain, and his amusement evaporated.

"Argh!"

He leapt around, but no amount of spinning and thrashing could dislodge the tiny mouse.

"Too!" Maldwyn cried.

Pinch slammed his tail to the floor. Her hold weakened.

Unmindful of his own well-being, Maldwyn threw himself at the cat, but he was too late.

With one whip-flick of his tail and a snap of his jaws, Too vanished.

Shock and a rising grief drove Maldwyn to such heights of fury that Pinch found himself in retreat. As he backed toward the stair landing, Maldwyn again flew at the cat—beak stabbing, claws tearing.

"Spit her out!" cried the raven.

CHAPTER FIFTY-SEVEN

Skilley left Pip with Nell and bounded into the chop room
on his way to the garret—only to discover the path to the
stairs blocked by a crowd of dumbfounded humans. He
chose a cautious route along the paneled wall.

He took a step forward.

Then another.

Then—

"Get back!" warned Henry.

At first Skilley thought the innkeeper was addressing him.

What followed, however, was a horrendous cawing
and snarling—and a rolling ball of black and ginger tumbled down the stairs and into the room.

The ball broke apart into…

    a cat…

        and a raven…

Each bearing evidence of blood upon him.

Skilley dashed between the two. He directed his long,
low *hisssssss* at Pinch.

"Maldwyn?" cried a man who clutched a slouch hat in
his hands. The raven, though hurt and dazed, cocked his
head and clacked his beak upon hearing his name.

The man advanced a step, but Pinch's snarling and clawing drove him back. From his pocket he produced a pistol.

"No!" shouted the woman in black. "You'll chance harming the bird." Then she turned an accusatory scowl on Henry. "How came you by a Tower raven?"

"I...I...I...," was all Henry could get out.

Pinch took a sideways lunge toward the raven.

But Skilley stepped forward and blocked his path. "Stay away from Maldwyn," he growled.

In response, Pinch snarled out a string of curses. If the humans could have understood them, his obscenities would have gained him his head on a pike, even in these enlightened times.

"You'll not bilk me out of me rights," Pinch spewed. "That bird is mine."

"He's certainly your match," mocked Skilley, "as he's half dead already."

"I'll take the other half if my hurrying him to St. Peter's will bring you grief..."

Skilley spied the quiver in Pinch's flank. Before the other humans could respond, Pinch leapt toward Maldwyn.

"The ginger cat!" warned the Queen. "He's for the raven!"

But Skilley was faster. He landed hard on Pinch, claws unsheathed, and knocked him to the floor. The two rolled through the sawdust, hissing and spitting.

This distraction gave the Ravenmaster a chance to scoop the raven up in his arms.

"Get back!" warned Mr. Dickens. "The cats are squaring off!"

"It's sick you make me," Pinch croaked. "Befriendin' birds and mice, and gawd knows what manner o' things. Things you'd be eatin' if you was a proper cat. I know

your filthy secret…" He scuttled away from Skilley, breathing heavily.

Now it was Skilley who paced back and forth, as if daring Pinch to attack again.

"You eat *cheese*." The words emerged from Pinch's clenched jaws with a slow hiss.

So, he knows.

Skilley allowed himself an instant of surprise to savor how little he now cared. "Yes. I eat cheese. What's more, my truest friend in this friendless world is a mouse. And I would risk my life for him, and for that bird—"

"Traitor!" slavered Pinch.

"Quick, stop them!" cried one of the humans.

"Not me," answered another. "I value me fingers."

Pinch leapt again.

This time, his insane anger gave him an unexpected strength and speed. Skilley dodged, but this was no fish-wife's broom. Pinch's claw raked his nose.

Another vicious swipe ripped into his shoulder.

Skilley cried out at the pain.

CHAPTER FIFTY-EIGHT

Nell emerged from the kitchen to join the other humans. Pip, upon hearing the horrendous snarls and shouts, struggled to peep over the top of her pocket. He saw immediately the insatiable loathing for Skilley that was driving Pinch beyond the bounds of all common sense. Pip had to help.

But how?

He thought back to the day he had watched in horror as Bodkin was devoured. The memory made him shudder. And it made him angry. Was he once again doomed to be a hapless witness at the death of a friend?

You're only a mere spark of a mouse, Pip.

Then another thought took hold.

If one mouse is a spark...then ten thousand mice are a conflagration.

"Don't worry, Skilley," he whispered. "We're coming."

Despite the burning pain in his hind leg, he crept from Nell's pocket and lowered himself, unseen, down her skirt.

"I've never eaten raven before. P'rhaps I'll start with his good eye," goaded Pinch. In his rage he hadn't noticed that Maldwyn was safely out of his reach.

Skilley slashed with his own paw, ripping a swath down Pinch's back. But his adversary was beyond feeling now. He frothed and foamed. He struck with venom, wrapping his claws around Skilley's neck.

"See," Pinch ground out, "I've just had a lovely mouse snack. You can smell the little 'un still on my breath."

Skilley struggled to free himself, but Pinch's hind claws dug into his stomach. "What little one?" he cried.

Pinch ignored the question. "You've never killed another cat before." His voice was like a razor, slashing through Skilley's nerves. "I *have*."

"What little one?" Skilley gasped as the claws dug deeper. He pushed and pulled, twisted and squirmed, but Pinch had an unbreakable grip.

"Too small for a name, it was," spat Pinch.

At that news, Skilley gave in to Pinch's grip.

No, no. Not Too.

Summoning the last of his strength, he wrenched his body forward and whispered, "As I suspected…a coward—"

Pinch responded with a plaster-cracking yowl. Not from the insult, but from a most real and most painful injury.

In his wrestling with Skilley, he'd backed against the chop room wall, where his posterior was stabbed by the sharp point of a nail. Even his thick hide could not resist that fateful spike of iron. He yowled again and dropped Skilley to the floor, who took advantage of Pinch's distress to scramble away.

His rage was volcanic as he rounded back on Skilley, not noticing the flicker of the gaslights.

But Skilley did.

They dimmed once.

Twice.

A third time.

Within moments the smell of musk was overpowering.

Everyone in the room froze.

And then

came...

the mice.

From every corner of the inn they came. They broke through plaster and pushed up through floorboards. Pip had given the ancient signal and they had answered.

They swarmed to Skilley's aid. Down the stairs they streamed, up from the cellar, through the ceiling, flowing like quicksilver along the walls and across the floor to encircle Skilley in a gray tide, all the while washing back Pinch, like so much flotsam, to the very feet of the humans.

"I 'ate these blasted mice!" screamed Pinch.

"I love these blessed mice!" sang Skilley.

"Indeed," cawed Maldwyn.

Humans leapt onto chairs or tables, except for the few who were rendered inert as they observed the mischief of mice with a mixture of wonder and dread.

An inspired madness had overtaken the room.

CHAPTER FIFTY-NINE

Pip looked about him at the sea of mice that
flooded the floor, the bar, the stairs. Its tide
drove back the snarling, spitting Pinch.
Like protective waters they
ebbed and flowed around
Skilley. The exhausted
cat crouched, licking
a nasty wound on

his shoulder. With a caw and an awkward flutter of wings, the Tower raven escaped the grasp of the Ravenmaster and flew to Skilley's side.

"Maldwyn!" the man commanded.

But the Tower raven knew his dues. He stood erect next to Skilley, looking every bit worthy of the dignity of his office, even with the patch of feathers missing from the middle of his forehead. Then he touched his beak ever so carefully to the cat's brow.

Thwarted, Pinch screamed out incoherent threats and insults, only identifiable as such by the timbre and pitch. He was joined in this madness by a gibbering wreck of a girl, whom some recognized as Adele, though others who knew her well had their doubts.

"Me cleaver!" she cried. "Where's me cleaver? I'll kill 'em all, like I done afore!" She tore at her hair. She ripped her apron to shreds. She stomped and kicked and slashed out at every mouse within reach. A double handful of coins tumbled from her torn pocket. "Me cheese money!" Flashes of gold and silver bounced and rolled across the floor to disappear beneath the gray carpet of mice. "That's mine! MINE!"

"It's you who's been stealing me cheese? And selling it!" cried Croomes.

"Adele? Selling our cheese?" echoed Henry.

As Adele inched toward the door, one of the Queen's men cast her a grim look and barred the exit.

Pinch chose that moment to release a long hiss.

The other humans backed away, giving him a wide berth. The cat made random swats at the air as if attacking a swarm of bees.

It was Mr. Dickens who braved the cat's insanity. He bent down and yanked him up by the scruff of the neck. Pinch immediately relaxed, not with calm, but rather as if his mind had simply disengaged itself and left his body to operate as best as it could, which is to say, not at all. The ginger cat hung motionless in Mr. Dickens's grip. A bit of frothy drool collected at the corners of his mouth.

The Ravenmaster made a hesitant move toward his charge. "Maldwyn," he called. "Are you alright, my boy?"

"Someone will pay for this crime," Queen Victoria said. "Oh, for the days of yore…" She shook her head. "But the headsman's ax has grown rusty and dull."

Henry gulped and tugged at his collar. "Your Majesty," he squeaked. "I truly don't know what…how…when…"

"I do." Nell pushed her way forward. The gray sea of mice parted and opened a path to the raven. She stepped carefully through and gently lifted Maldwyn in her arms.

"Careful, young miss," cried his master. "Maldwyn can give you a nasty—" He stared in awe to see how docile the raven was in her hand. "Well, upon my word."

Nell carried Maldwyn directly back to him. "I rescued him once," she explained, "before I'd been sent to the country. He was being mauled by cats. I heard the frightful noise and ran to the alley. The cats fled when they saw me. And my friends the mice helped me nurse the raven back to health, though I'm afraid he'll never fly again."

She settled the raven into the man's arms.

"He weren't supposed to be flyin' in the first place." The Ravenmaster gave the bird a severe look.

At last, Henry spoke. "My daughter has always had a winning way with animals." Pausing to cast a guilty glance toward Nell, he added, "And after this day I'll never disbelieve her again—"

"Is this story true?" asked the Queen.

"Oh, yes," admitted Henry. "Nell could tame a wild—"

"Merciful heavens! Will someone awaken me from this lunacy? I was inquiring about the raven."

"Seems it's so." The Ravenmaster examined the three scars across Maldwyn's eye. "Besides these new wounds, he bears older marks of teeth and claws."

"B-b-but t-t-the m-m-mice!" Adele stuttered with sobs and gasps. "Does no one care that this place is a wretched den of rodents?"

"Indeed," Queen Victoria said. "I've never seen such an infestation. I do believe you're in want of arsenic."

"Wait!" interrupted Mr. Dickens and Croomes together.

After a surprised glance at the cook, Mr. Dickens went on. "Er…begging your pardon, but does Your Majesty not see what's happened here?" He held out the disgraced cat.

"Our raven is safe," the Queen said. "What has the rest of it to do with Our Person?"

Mr. Dickens seemed to put a great deal of store in his position as a writer, for he pressed the royal lady. "Is it not evident? This cat was trying to kill Your Majesty's raven." He handed off the subdued beast to one of the Queen's men. "The raven was saved by the blue cat. The cat that has just been saved by"—he cast his hand out over the sea of mice—"these creatures. The very ones who cared for your raven when he was attacked once before, as young Nell has just testified."

Queen Victoria took a moment to examine the scene. Slowly, she allowed the events of the previous minutes to take on a different meaning.

"You can't mean for Us to think—"The Queen's eyes fell on an agitated mouse. As he pressed against the swell of his fellow creatures, a narrow corridor began to open. The Queen fixed her attention firmly on the mouse, and everyone else in the room obediently followed her gaze.

Within seconds, a curious silence befell the company as they watched a limping Pip reach his friend, who lay panting in a corner of the room. Paying no heed to his audience, Pip clambered onto Skilley's shoulder and began to clean his wound.

"But this is…it can't be…it's…," stammered the Queen. "Are you proposing, sir, that a cat and mouse—historic enemies—can live together in friendship?"

"I have great expectations," said Mr. Dickens.

CHAPTER SIXTY

A distressed Henry interrupted. "But whatever am I to do with the rest of these rodents?"

"Thank your stars for them," said Mr. Dickens. "Not only have they assisted in the rescue of a Tower raven, but I have a certain suspicion..." He scratched a hand through his groomed beard as if searching for the right words. "Fetch me a bit of your Cheshire," he said to Henry. Then he turned to Queen Victoria. "Your Majesty," he said. "May I entreat you to taste the most excellent cheese in England?"

Henry brightened when he realized what Mr. Dickens had asked. He glanced down at the cheese that had broken when Adele flung the cloth-wrapped wheel at the wall.

"Something a bit fresher, perhaps?" suggested Mr. Dickens in a low tone.

Henry nodded and bounded to the stairs.

"This is nonsense," Queen Victoria said. "My dairy in Windsor produces a most satisfactory variety."

"I implore Your Majesty but to taste it," Dickens said.

Henry returned with a slab of gold.

It was strange to see the Queen accept a piece of cheese

handed to her by a common innkeeper. But then, the entire affair had been odd. And it was not yet concluded.

Henry handed her the slab. She ate the whole thing. And asked for another.

"Wonderful cheese, is it not?" asked Mr. Dickens.

"I've never tasted its like," she answered. "How is it possible?" She turned to Henry. "What is your secret?"

Henry in turn applied to Croomes, who shrugged her massive shoulders. "An old family receipt," she said rather mysteriously. And she lifted her eyes to the ceiling, as if inspecting it for signs of cracks.

Mr. Dickens, himself the creator of many an outrageous fiction, shook his head. "It's more than that, I believe. It's the mice, isn't it, Agnes? With taste-testers such as these, how could the recipe go amiss?" Although he smiled, his eyes bored into Croomes like two augers.

"Wha—?" Henry looked from Mr. Dickens to his cook. It had been a wild gamble on the writer's part, and it paid off handsomely.

Agnes Croomes's round face turned the shade of pickled beets. "True enough. And why should I not rely on them what knows best?" No one answered, so she continued unchecked. "I peer in on each new batch of cheese after it's aged a few months in the cellar. If the mice 'ave been at it, I know it's a fine batch. They'll not touch a mediocre Cheshire. We've only the most persnickety mice here at the Cheese."

"And if they turn up their noses at it, then what?" demanded an astounded Henry.

Croomes turned to the Queen with pride and announced, "We sells it to the French."

Charles Dickens

CHAPTER SIXTY-ONE

"Ahem!" Queen Victoria cleared her throat, and the laughter that had been the result of Croomes's announcement instantly died.

From her post near the door, Adele gave the Queen a cloying curtsey.

The Queen responded with a chilling look. In a voice just loud enough for all to hear, she announced, "We believe this young woman is in need of a reformatory. Red Lodge in Bristol will do nicely."

"Your Majesty!" wailed Adele.

One of the Queen's men was instantly at Adele's side. Taking her firmly by the arm, he led her outside, adding in a soothing tone, "They've plenty of mice at Red Lodge, miss…you'll feel right at home…"

"Ruin. Ruin, and penury. Are these to be our fate?" muttered a woeful Henry.

"If there are to be no further revelations," the Queen continued, casting a severe glance over all assembled, "We should like to make a proclamation in light of this day's most unorthodox events."

The Queen addressed the crowd:

"Let it be known that the mice of Ye Olde Cheshire Cheese are henceforth under Our Royal protection, as befitting the guardians of the finest cheese in the realm. Furthermore, so long as a single mouse resides at this inn, its doors shall never close."

It was a moment that encouraged extravagance.

Ten thousand mice cheered.

Mr. Dickens took a blushing Croomes in his arms and led her around the room in a reel.

Nell slipped an affectionate arm around her portly father.

The innkeeper looked down at her. "Its doors shall never close...," he whispered, dizzy with delight.

And they never have.

EPILOGUE

Some few days following the Queen's visit to the inn, Pip found Skilley on the rooftop. The rain had swept toward the continent to bluster and blow across the innocent French countryside.

"I was just coming for you," said a sleepy Skilley as he lazily stretched one leg, then another.

"Yes, well."

Pip licked his paw…

stroked his ear…

licked his paw…

and touched his nose.

"Are you still fretting about Too?" asked Skilley with a touch of irritation. "She'll soon learn to get about on three legs. And it seems to me that she's positively relishing her role as heroine—"

"No, I'm certain that Too will be fine," said Pip. Still, he allowed a final shiver of stale fear to pass through him. It had been beyond anyone's hope to see little Too again. Yet they had found her, weak but alive, in a bloody corner of the garret landing. The very memory sent Pip into a frenzy of ablution: he licked both paws at once and began to vigorously scrub at his face.

"Gadzooks, Pip!" cried Skilley, his concern mounting. "Will you tell me what's wrong?"

"It's our mutual friend, Mr. Dickens."

"Dickens?" Skilley was dumbfounded. "Why, thanks to him the inn is safe, and so are the mice. He's no doubt even now scribbling away—"

"He is not scribbling away, Skilley! He's not slept for days, for want of knowing what to scribble!"

"Say again?"

"He lacks a beginning for his story."

Skilley coiled and uncoiled his tail as he stared at Pip in rapt attention. "And just how would you know this?"

"I-I read his papers," Pip confessed. "Oh, Skilley! It's the most marvelous tale of two cities—"

"You what? You read his papers! After what you said about reading a writer's—"

"But Skilley, now that I know what's been troubling our Mr. Dickens"—Pip beamed a smile that showed his excellent teeth to greatest advantage—"I believe I may have found a small way to thank him for his kindness…"

C. DICKENS

It was the best of times,
It was the worst of times

We hope you have enjoyed THE CHESHIRE CHEESE CAT. Included here are definitions for some words that may be new to you. In the event that we missed a few, we suggest a trip to the dictionary, a pastime that we find most enjoyable. For more details about Charles Dickens, the Tower ravens, or Ye Olde Cheshire Cheese, you can visit our website at www.cheshirecheesecat.com.

Carmen Agra Deedy and Randall Wright

GLOSSARY

abject—very low in spirit or hope

ablution—washing or bathing

ague—chills, fever, and sweating; the flu

apathy—lack of feeling or caring

apoplexy—a stroke caused by a brain hemorrhage; an angry fit

audacity—daring; reckless boldness

auger—a spiral-shaped sharp-pointed tool used for boring holes

bellows—a device for pumping air onto a weak fire to make it stronger

black pudding—sausage made from blood

brigand—a bandit; a thief

bubble and squeak—cabbage fried with potatoes and sometimes meat

caterwaul—to utter a yowling cry

char-room—the place where cleaning supplies are stored

choleric—angry; likely to throw nasty fits of temper

chummery—time spent chumming about with one's chums

churlish—rude, surly

claret—a kind of wine

cloying—excessively sweet

congenial—friendly

consternation—confused amazement; dismay

counterpane—a bedspread

culinary—having to do with cooking

curmudgeon—an ill-tempered and stubborn person

drivel—nonsense; stupid or careless talk

dropsy—a medical condition where fluid is retained in tissues and joints

dumbwaiter—a small elevator for moving food and other items
  between floors

dyspepsia—heartburn; ill humor

elixir—a cure-all; a medicinal concoction

erstwhile—former; in the past

filbert—a hazelnut

flatulence—the state of having digestive gas
  (Yes, this is what you think it is.)

flotsam—the floating wreckage of a ship

gastronomic—having to do with the art and science of good eating

gob—a patterer's word for "mouth"

gout—a form of arthritis, often caused by the overeating of rich foods

ha-penny—short for "halfpenny," which, in turn, is short for "half a penny"

hansom cab—a two-wheeled horse buggy that seats two people and a driver

hugger-mugger—British street talk for cloak and dagger secrecy; confusion

imperious—behaving like someone who is a supreme ruler

insatiable—impossible to satisfy

irony—the use of words that mean the opposite of what one really intends

kith and kin—friends and relatives, in that order

languid—lacking force or quickness of movement

lexicographical—having to do with the making of a dictionary

moggy—British street slang for a tomcat

nether—lower

palsy—a medical condition marked by uncontrollable shaking
 or partial paralysis

patter—the specialized language of street vendors or of certain criminals

peckish—hungry, sometimes to the point of irritation

penury—extreme poverty

perfidy—treachery; betrayal

perfunctory—halfhearted; done mechanically or carelessly

pernicious—very destructive; deadly

posthaste—quickly; with great speed

preposterous—unbelievable; nonsensical

prismatic—highly colored, brilliant; like the colors made by a prism

prodigious—huge; unusual

quicksilver—the common word for the element mercury

rapacious—greedy or predatory

recalcitrant—unyielding; stubbornly refusing to give in to authority

repast—a meal

rumination—a thought

scrivener—a professional copyist or writer; a scribe

skullduggery—dishonest behavior; trickery

soliloquy—the act of talking to oneself

squeamish—easily sickened, shocked, or disgusted

stillroom—a pantry where jams and jellies are kept

stygian—pitch dark, like the River Styx in the mythological underworld

treacle—British word for molasses

trepidation—a state of alarm or nervousness

trundle—to move on or as if on wheels

tryst—a secret meeting

tuppence—British two-penny coin

turgid—being in a swollen state

unabsolved—not forgiven

unorthodox—out of the ordinary; not usual

volatile—likely to change quickly or suddenly

waxing—growing larger, stronger, fuller, or more numerous

whiffle—to blow

wraithlike—ghostly

A SMATTERING OF PATTERING
Patterers' words from Mr. Dickens's notebook

balamy—insane; eventually shortened to "balmy"
hookem-snivey—trickery
milch—to trick
snilch—to eye over carefully
thimblejigger—a trickster; literally, an expert at the pea and shell game
toff—a fine gentleman
whiddler—an informer or betrayer

Text is typeset in Joanna, designed by Eric Gill
and released by the Monotype Foundry in 1937.
Charles Dickens's journal pages are typeset in Adobe's Poetica Chancery III.
Pip's handwriting is typeset in Emmascript by Kanna Aoki, who drew the letters
while picnicking in San Francisco's Golden Gate Park, and her writing
was adapted as a font by Mark van Bronkhorst.
Title is typeset in Monotype Foundry's Gloucester MT Extra Condensed,
based on a design created in 1896 by Bertram G. Goodhue.